Beneath Southern Stars

A Novel of the Reaver, the Sea, And the Love That Refused to Drown.

By

Sophie Jane

Sophie Jane

Copyright © 2026 Sophie Jane

All rights reserved.

No part of this publication may be reproduced, stored in a retrieval system, or transmitted in any form or by any means, electronic, mechanical, photocopying, recording, or otherwise, without prior written permission of the copyright owner, except in the case of brief quotations used in reviews or articles.

Published by:

Dedication

For my daughters — my greatest adventure.

May you grow up with hearts as wild as the Western coastline

and spirits as strong as the desert sun.

Protect the magic you find.

Chase the stories that call you.

And never let a secret disappear

if it deserves to be lived boldly to its end.

Sophie Jane

Acknowledgment

This story was born from salt air, long horizons, and the quiet pull of the sea.

To my daughters — you are the reason I write, the reason I dream, and the reason I believe in brave endings. May you always chase the tide with courage and hold love as fiercely as the ocean holds its secrets.

To my family, who have listened to endless talk of ships, storms, and stubborn captains — thank you for believing in this story even when it existed only as scattered notes and restless thoughts. Your support has been my anchor.

To those who walk beside me in real life — the adventurers, the risk-takers, the quiet encouragers — thank you for reminding me that stories are not just written, they are lived.

To the wild Western Australian coastline — the cliffs, the wind, the Sound, and the islands that feel untouched by time — you shaped every page. This book carries your breath in it.

While Beneath Southern Stars is a work of fiction, it is inspired by the real life and legend of Jack Anderson, whose story is woven into the wild history of the archipelago. Though time has scattered truth and myth alike, his name — and the spirit of those untamed waters — will not go untold.

And finally, to the sea itself — for teaching me that love, like tide, always returns.

With gratitude and salt in my veins,

Sophie Jane

Table of Contents

Chapter One:
Tempest Rising

The sea was a sheet of glass when Ava Lawson cut the engine.

She let her tinny drift with the current, the outboard's hum fading until the only sound was the ocean's whisper — a lazy hush against the hull. Late afternoon light gilded the Recherche Archipelago, painting the chain of islands in molten gold. Granite peaks rose sharp and jagged from the water, like the backs of sleeping sea monsters.

Ava tipped her cap against the glare and raised her binoculars. A colony of Australian sea lions sprawled across a slick outcrop just ahead, their golden hides gleaming wetly under the sun. She smiled, jotting notes quickly in her waterproof journal, the pencil scratching between gusts of salt air.

"Perfect," she murmured. "Tag, release, back by six. Easy."

She should have known better. The ocean never did "easy."

The wind shifted first — a sharp, cold bite sweeping in from the southwest. Ava froze. She'd been on the water long enough to understand the language of these seas. This was a warning.

Her gaze shot to the horizon.

The sky, moments ago a brilliant wash of pink and orange, had turned bruised and heavy. A black wall of cloud stretched wide, curling like the lip of a monstrous wave.

"Shit," she hissed.

She started the outboard and turned for Esperance. The islands that had seemed so idyllic now loomed like jagged sentinels, cliffs dark and slick, ready to chew up anything foolish enough to come too close.

The first raindrops were fat and cold, splattering against her skin.

Then came the wind — sharp, violent, snatching at her hair and shirt. The swells rose fast, black water heaving beneath the tinny, tossing it like it weighed nothing.

"Esperance base, this is Lawson," she called into the radio. "Storm rolling in. Heading in now. Over."

Static. Nothing.

"Bloody perfect."

The sea had stopped playing nice.

A wall of water slammed into the bow, drenching her in icy spray. The boat pitched skyward, then crashed into the trough with a bone-jarring thud. Thunder rolled overhead, lightning flashing stark against reefs just metres away.

"Not today," she spat, wrestling the wheel. Her arms burned as she fought the current dragging her towards the rocks.

Another crash. A sharp crack — metal on stone, shuddered through the tinny. Panic flared. One more hit like that and she was done.

And then… silence. A hollow pause between thunder and lightning.

That's when she saw it.

At first, just a smudge in the rain. Then, a silhouette. A ship.

Not a trawler. Not a research vessel. A ship.

Black from bow to stern, its hull knifed through the swell, sails taut in the gale. Lightning flared again, rigging gleamed silver, and men — shadows , moved swiftly across the deck.

Ava blinked salt from her lashes. "No… no, that's—"

The ship bore down. Her battered tinny didn't stand a chance.

Then she saw him.

At the helm, towering over the storm, a man. Broad-shouldered, rain running over dark leather straps, a cutlass at his hip. The storm seemed to bend around him. Lightning flashed in steel-grey eyes that locked on her with predator focus.

The ship veered hard. A rope snapped through the air, slapping wet against her deck.

"Grab it!"

The voice — deep, rough, with a cadence of old oceans: part Caribbean lilt, part Cape roll, timeless. It curled with command, the kind that made her fingers move before her brain caught up.

"No bloody way—"

The wave swallowed her protest. She seized the rope, slick with rain, and the world lurched sideways.

With one brutal pull, the stranger hauled her across the gap. She slammed into the ship's side, then strong hands lifted her onto slick timber.

Ava coughed seawater from her lungs, shoved hair out of her face, and froze.

The man loomed above her, rain dripping from dark, unruly hair, his jaw cut sharp. His storm-grey gaze swept over her, unreadable.

"Welcome aboard, Red," he said, voice low and dangerous. "Looks like you've just bought a ticket you can't refund."

Ava shoved wet hair out of her face, her chest burning with adrenaline. "Who the hell are you?"

He studied her, eyes narrowing, then curved his mouth in something that wasn't quite a smile.

"Alive," he said. "For now. You're welcome."

She barked a laugh. "Oh, right. Thanks for the kidnapping. Five stars. Would recommend."

"Kidnapping?" His voice cooled, sharp as a blade. "I pulled you from a grave. You want to go back in, I'll oblige."

A shiver chased down her spine, but she held her ground. "Red? My name's Ava. And I didn't ask for your help."

"You didn't need to." His eyes held hers, storm-grey and unyielding. "Sea was chewing you up. One more wave, and you'd be a ghost story."

Ghost story. The word landed heavier than it should have. Locals loved their tales — pirates, smugglers, Black Jack Anderson, the so-called ghost who once ruled these waters. Ava had laughed them off as bar chatter. Until now.

"What is this?" she demanded, waving at the ropes, the brass, the black sails snapping overhead. "Cosplay? Pirates of the Southern Ocean?"

The crew snorted. The man didn't blink.

"You're in no position to mock, Red." He leaned closer, rain brushing her temple. "And this ship? She's as real as the bones you'd be feeding the sharks."

Her voice steadied. "Then maybe tell me why you dragged me aboard your ghost ship instead of dropping me at the marina."

His mouth twitched, almost a smile.

"Because, Ava Lawson," he said, tasting her name, "you and I are going to have a little chat. And when we're done..." His gaze sharpened. "...you'll tell me everything you know about Black Jack Anderson."

She stared. "Black Jack—what? He's a legend. A ghost story."

Lightning split the sky, illuminating his face. What flickered in his eyes wasn't disbelief.

"Ghost stories," he murmured, "are always built on truth."

Chapter Two:
The Night Reaver

The ship pitched and groaned as it carved through the storm, black sails straining against the howling wind. Lanterns swung wildly in their brackets, throwing jagged shadows across the deck.

Ava braced herself against the mast, rain stinging her cheeks as she watched the stranger — take the helm with terrifying calm. His movements were precise, controlled, as if the chaos around them didn't exist.

She hated that it made her stare.

And she hated even more that her pulse still hadn't settled.

When the sea finally began to ease, the rain thinning to a fine mist, the first bite of cold sank into her bones. She wrapped her arms around herself, teeth chattering.

"Oi."

A voice at her shoulder — low, sharp. She turned to find a young deckhand, no older than twenty, holding out a dry blanket. He looked nervous, like even standing this close might earn him a flogging.

"Captain says you'll catch your death without this," he mumbled.

She took it with stiff fingers, muttering a quick, "Thanks," before her eyes slid back to the captain.

The man — Dante, she'd overheard one of the crew call him — stood with his back to her, broad shoulders rigid as he adjusted the ship's course. Lightning flickered along the horizon, illuminating the sharp planes of his face when he finally turned, eyes locking on hers.

"Inside," he said, voice low but carrying enough weight to silence the crew.

Ava's brows shot up. "Excuse me?"

"Below deck." He strode toward her, boots striking the slick planks with purpose. "You're freezing, you're soaked, and you're no good to anyone if you collapse."

"No good to anyone?" She planted her feet, ignoring the tremor in her hands. "I didn't ask to be here. Drop me at Esperance, and we'll call it even."

Dante stopped inches from her, close enough that she caught the scent of salt and storm on his skin, and something sharper beneath it.

"Not happening," he said. "Not until we talk."

Ava tilted her chin, summoning every ounce of stubbornness. "Talk about what?"

The corner of his mouth ticked — not amusement, exactly, but something darker. "About the man whose name I said on deck. Black Jack Anderson."

She scoffed, clutching the blanket tighter. "Look, Captain Broody—"

One of the crew choked on a laugh. Dante's head turned slowly, and the deckhand suddenly found a coil of rope fascinating.

"You think this is a joke," Dante said, quieter now — quieter, and far more dangerous. "But where we're headed, there's no room for jokes."

"And where is that, exactly?" Ava shot back. "Some treasure island fantasy? You do realise the man you're chasing has been dead for two hundred years, right?"

For a heartbeat, she thought he might smile — but there was no humour in it, only steel.

"Dead men leave trails," Dante said. "And if I'm right, you've been studying one without even knowing it."

Her stomach twisted. "I don't know what you're talking about."

"Oh, you do, Red." His eyes narrowed, sharp as glass. "Those reefs you've been mapping? Those coordinates you've sent to the mainland? They're not just dots on a chart. They're markers. Keys."

Ava blinked at him, thrown. "Keys to what?"

The deck rocked as the ship rode another swell, pitching her — straight into his chest. His hands caught her elbows, rough palms steadying her. For a heartbeat, the storm was silent — nothing but the heat of his grip, the closeness, the weight of his gaze.

Then he released her, stepping back as though burned.

"To something you don't want to be in the middle of," he said flatly. "But it's too late for that now."

The *Night Reaver* cut through the restless sea, her black hull gleaming like obsidian under fractured moonlight. The storm had eased to a drizzle, but the deck still groaned under every swell, the ship alive beneath Ava's feet.

She clutched the blanket tighter, damp hair plastered to her cheek. The man at the helm — Dante, she'd gathered from the way the others spoke his name — hadn't looked her way since dragging her aboard. Not once.

Fine by her.

Except it wasn't fine. Not when her heart still hadn't slowed.

"Storm'll break by morning," a voice said to her left.

Ava turned. A tall, rangy man leaned against the rail, rope coiled over one shoulder. His skin was bronzed, dark curls plastered to his forehead, his smile easy, almost enough to disguise the sharp watchfulness in his eyes.

"Rafi," he said, offering a hand. "Navigator. And unofficial peacemaker, when the Captain gets all broody."

Ava raised a brow but shook his hand. "Ava. Unofficial hostage, apparently."

Rafi chuckled, shaking his head. "Don't take it personal, love. Storm like that, you were lucky he spotted you. Lucky he pulled you in."

"Lucky," Ava repeated dryly. "Right. Because being dragged onto a ghost ship in the middle of nowhere screams good luck."

Rafi's grin widened. "Ghost ship, eh? You've got spirit. Careful with that. The Captain doesn't take well to people poking at his shadows."

From the companionway, a woman's voice cut through the hum of the deck: sharp, crisp, and laced with a lilting accent Ava couldn't quite place.

"Rafi, stop flirting with the stray and get her below before she freezes solid."

Ava blinked as the woman strode over, a first-aid kit tucked under one arm. She was striking, tall and lean, with dark hair braided tight and eyes like cut glass.

"Isla," Rafi said, rolling his eyes. "Our medic. Ignore her bark. She only bites when you bleed on her deck."

"I'll bite if you keep running your mouth," Isla shot back, then gave Ava a brisk once-over. "You hurt?"

"No," Ava said quickly. "Just... cold. Confused. And very ready to get back to the mainland."

Isla's expression didn't soften. "You'll find your bearings. Or you won't. Either way, follow me — and don't touch anything."

Below deck, the ship was a maze of narrow corridors and warm lamplight. The air smelled of salt, wood, and something spiced — rum, maybe, or cloves. Isla led her into a small cabin: sparse but clean. A cot bolted to the wall. A single porthole.

"This'll do," Isla said, setting the kit on the desk. "Get dry. Sleep. And if you want to live through this, stay out of Dante's way until he decides what to do with you."

Ava stiffened. "Decides what to do with me? I didn't ask to be here."

"Doesn't matter." Isla's gaze was cool, unreadable. "Nothing happens on this ship unless Dante Vance allows it. Best remember that."

The door clicked shut, leaving Ava in the dim, swaying room, every nerve strung tight.

Above deck, Dante stood at the bow, one hand on his cutlass, eyes on the horizon.

"She's not just some stray," Isla said quietly, stepping up beside him.

"No," Dante agreed, voice low. "She's the key to Anderson's trail. Whether she knows it or not."

Hours later, Ava lay in the narrow bunk, the ship rocking gently beneath her. She tried to sleep, tried to ignore the murmur of voices above, the creak of timber, the distant hiss of waves.

But every time she closed her eyes, all she saw were storm-grey eyes locking on hers.

And the way he'd said her name, like it was something dangerous.

Chapter Three:
Smoke and Salt

The dream came on like the storm.

Ava was back on deck, rain in her hair, sea spray on her lips. But the ship wasn't bucking and heaving beneath her — it was steady, thrumming, alive. Lantern light flickered gold across dark wood, and the night was thick with salt and something sharper, something that burned all the way down.

He was there.

Dante.

He moved like the ship belonged to him, every step deliberate, every inch of space claimed. Storm-grey eyes, sharp as steel, caught hers across the deck and held until her knees threatened to buckle.

"You shouldn't be here," he said, voice low, dangerous.

"I didn't ask to be," she snapped — though her voice shook, and she hated that he'd hear it.

He came closer, boots whispering against the slick planks, until the world narrowed to the heat of his body and the wild thrum of her pulse.

"Then why," he murmured, breath brushing her ear, "can't you seem to stay away, Red?"

His hands found her waist, rough palms pressing through damp fabric, his thumb tracing the line of her hip, the scrape of calloused skin against damp fabric sending a shock straight through her. She should have pulled back. Should have said something sharp, clever — sharpened her tongue, but her body betrayed her, leaning into him, breath caught, heartbeat surging.

The heat of his chest. The promise in the curl of his fingers, just shy of claiming—

Ava jolted awake, heart pounding like a drum in her chest.

For a moment she couldn't breathe. The dim cabin tilted with the ship's gentle roll, shadows swaying in lantern light. Her skin still burned, cheeks flushed with something sharp and unfamiliar.

"Get it together," she muttered, shoving damp hair from her face.

But the dream clung to her, his voice, that impossible heat— curling around her like smoke as she swung her legs out of the bunk and shoved her bare feet into her boots.

Above deck, the world had changed.

The storm had burned itself out overnight, leaving the sea deceptively calm — a sheet of deep blue stretching toward the endless horizon. The sun was sharp and bright, scattering diamonds across the water. The *Night Reaver* cut through the swell like a predator, sleek and certain, sails snapping clean in the breeze.

Ava stepped onto the deck and breathed it in, the tang of brine and tar, men hauling lines, the creak of rigging. A place out of time, yet alive in every detail.

And every pair of eyes was on her.

The weight of their stares prickled her spine, but she refused to shrink. Chin lifted her chin, her gaze skimming the deck until it landed on him.

Dante.

At the helm, shirt open at the throat, dark hair damp with spray. Sunlight caught the planes of his face, the hard lines of his jaw, the casual authority in the way he stood. He didn't look at her right away.

But he knew.

She felt it.

Ava squared her shoulders and marched across the deck, boots striking hard against the planks.

"We need to talk," she said, sharp enough to slice through the hum of work around them.

One brow rose lazily as his gaze swept her, from damp hair to clenched fists. "Morning to you too, Red."

She ignored the nickname, planting herself in front of him. "You're going to turn this ship around. Now. You've had your fun, your... whatever this is. But I have a job. A life. And I'm not your—"

"Hostage?" His voice was quiet, but it carried.

"Yes," she snapped. "Hostage. And you're going to—"

Before she could finish, Dante moved. Not quickly, but with a controlled precision that made her breath hitch. He stepped in, close enough that the warmth of his body wrapped around her despite the sharp morning breeze, close enough that the world narrowed to storm-grey eyes and the steady thrum of the ship beneath her feet.

"You think you understand what's happening here," he said, low and almost gentle. "But you don't. You don't know these waters, you don't know this hunt, and you sure as hell don't know what's coming."

"I don't care," she shot back, pulse hammering in her ears. "I didn't ask to be part of your little pirate game."

His jaw tightened. He leaned close, enough that his next words brushed her ear.

"This isn't a game, Ava."

The way he said her name, low, deliberate, almost reverent, sent a sharp shiver down her spine.

The silence stretched, taut as a rope straining against the tide, until a voice rang out across the deck.

"Land on the horizon!"

Dante's gaze cut away, sharp, assessing. "Rafi, hold her steady," he barked, then turned back to Ava, his expression unreadable.

"You want off my ship?" His voice was calm now, but carried weight. "Help me find what I'm looking for. Then, and only then — I'll see you back to Esperance."

Ava opened her mouth to argue, but the words withered when she caught the flicker in his eyes. Not cruelty, but something harder. Older.

Whatever this was, it wasn't just about her anymore.

Chapter Four:
Ghosts of the Archipelago

The Recherche Archipelago stretched out before them like scattered emeralds, each island carved sharp by wind and tide, each cloaked in secrets. Hundreds of rocks and islets, every one holding a fragment of this ancient granite seascape.

By midday, the *Night Reaver* slipped through a channel narrow enough to taste the salt off the stone. Sun blazed overhead, turning the water into fractured turquoise, breaking white against jagged reefs.

Ava leaned against the rail, eyes narrowed on the nearest island. From here, it looked wild, untouched, a slice of land frozen in time.

"You'll want boots," a voice rumbled behind her.

She didn't need to turn. That voice, gravel wrapped in velvet, with a strange lilt caught between South Africa and the Caribbean — was unmistakable.

She turned toward him. Dante stood there, one hand on the rigging, shirt sleeves rolled to his elbows. The sunlight caught the scars that crossed his forearms, the ink curling over tanned skin like whispers of another life.

"Why?" she asked, folding her arms. "Afraid I'll ruin your perfect deck?"

A corner of his mouth twitched, almost, but not quite, a smile. "Afraid the rocks'll ruin you, Red. Those islands aren't made for the unprepared."

She bristled at the nickname but let it go this time. Maybe because the island ahead tugged at her in ways she couldn't explain.

After a beat, she said, "I know this place. Well… the stories, anyway."

That made him look at her properly.

"My dad used to tell me about him. Black Jack Anderson." Her gaze drifted toward the horizon, the shimmer of waves striking jagged stone. "The only pirate to ever call Australia home. The boogeyman of these islands. He said Anderson knew the waters like they were in his blood, buried treasure where only the ocean herself could guard it."

Dante's eyes narrowed, not with anger, but with something that looked like curiosity. A flicker of something deeper.

"And what else did your father say?"

Ava shrugged, though her throat tightened. "That he was a monster. Ruthless. Dangerous. That he ruled the archipelago like a king until the sea swallowed him whole." She hesitated, voice dropping. "But I never believed the scary parts. Not all of them, anyway. People don't become legends unless someone's trying to control the story."

Dante stepped closer, the deck shifting beneath his boots. He leaned against the rail beside her, gaze fixed on the horizon.

"They got some of it right," he said quietly. "He was dangerous. Ruthless, when it mattered. But not the monster they painted him. Black Jack… he wanted freedom. More than anything. These islands were the only place he ever found it."

Ava studied him, the hard cut of his profile, the way the wind tugged at his dark hair. "And you?" she asked softly. "What are you chasing, Dante? Freedom? Treasure? Or just someone else's ghost?"

His gaze cut to hers, storm-grey and steady. For a moment, she thought he wouldn't answer.

Then, quiet as the tide: "All of it. And none of it. I owe him my life. If there's even a chance his bones are still out here, I'll find him. I have to."

There was something raw in his voice, something that hummed between them like a current.

Ava swallowed hard. "My dad used to say the sea doesn't give up her dead. That if you go looking for ghosts, you might just find yourself instead. And why would you owe an old pirate your life anyway?"

Dante huffed a humourless laugh, ignoring the question. "Then let's hope I like what I find."

It made her even more curious, about his ventures and this old ship she was pulled upon.

For a moment, neither moved. The silence stretched, taut and intimate, broken only by the slap of waves against the hull.

Behind them, Rafi's voice rang out, calling for the crew to drop anchor. The *Night Reaver* slowed, sails snapping as the island loomed closer, sharp cliffs, narrow beaches, gulls wheeling overhead.

Dante straightened first, pulling away from the moment. "Stay close," he said, warmth gone from his tone, replaced with steel. "These islands don't forgive mistakes."

Ava lifted her chin, matching his coolness even as something restless stirred in her chest. "Then you'd better keep up."

They lowered the longboat. The sea glittered like broken glass as they rowed toward shore. Ava trailed her hand through the water, the dream from the night before slipping unbidden into her mind — the heat, the weight of his hands, the sharpness of his voice.

She shook it off, fixing on the jagged silhouette of the island ahead. Whatever this journey was, it was pulling her deeper with every mile.

And she wasn't sure she wanted to fight it anymore.

Chapter Five:
The Island of Bones

The longboat scraped against the white sand with a sharp hiss, the sound almost deafening against the oppressive silence that clung to the island.

Ava stepped out carefully, her boots sinking into the damp sand. The place felt wrong. The air was thicker here, heavy with the tang of salt and something darker, a coppery, metallic undertone that curled in her stomach and made her breath shallow.

Behind her, Dante jumped down, landing with quiet, feline grace, his cutlass already strapped tight at his hip. Isla and Rafi followed, moving like they'd done this a hundred times before.

The jungle loomed ahead, wild and twisted, a wall of gnarled tea trees and pale eucalyptus trunks disappearing into shadow.

'Stay close,' Dante said, voice a low growl.

Ava bristled. 'I'm not a child.'

'No,' he said, eyes sharp as the edge of his blade, 'but this island doesn't care. One wrong step and you won't see the second one coming.'

The deeper they went, the darker it grew. The canopy above knitted together, blocking out the sun until only slivers of pale light pierced through. Every snap of a twig underfoot seemed to echo.

Rafi glanced back at her as he adjusted the rope slung over his shoulder. 'Feels different when you're standing on it, huh? Like the stories have teeth.'

Ava blinked at him. 'Stories?'

'About Anderson,' he said, voice low but edged with reverence, maybe even fear. 'They say he was last seen out here near the Recherche, what, Cap? Hundred and fifty years ago?'

'Hundred and eighty,' Dante corrected without looking back. His hand brushed the low branches as they walked, steady and sure. 'Last recorded sighting was 1835. Then nothing.'

'Nothing,' Isla echoed, keeping her rifle loose at her side. 'Just his ghost stamped all over these islands.'

Ava frowned, quickening her pace to keep up. 'But… what happened to him? Every version I heard as a kid ended differently.'

'Because no one knows,' Rafi said. 'Some say one of his own crew put a bullet in him, a mutiny gone sour. Others swear the women he kept, slaves, stolen from the mainland and other ships, slit his throat in his sleep and dumped him in a trench.'

'Others,' Dante added quietly, 'say he went mad. Walked into the sea one night and never came back. The ocean keeps its secrets, Red.'

Ava shivered despite the heavy, sticky air.

They stepped into a clearing, and Ava froze.

Time had not been kind here.

The skeleton of what must have been a shelter, a crude hut, maybe once a lookout post, leaned drunkenly at the edge of the clearing. Only warped timbers and rusted iron nails remained, jutting from the sand like jagged teeth. A coil of half-buried rope sat half-fused with coral and grit, as though the island itself was trying to swallow the remnants whole.

Then she saw it, the stone.

A dark slab half-hidden by overgrown scrub. Someone had carved deep into its surface, the grooves uneven but deliberate: a skull, crowned by a jagged line like lightning.

Her heart tripped in her chest. 'That's, '

'Anderson's mark,' Dante said, voice unreadable as he crouched before it. He ran gloved fingers along the grooves, brushing away clumps of moss. 'Still sharp. Older than it should be, but…' He exhaled slowly. 'This is him. This is his ground.'

'How old is it?' Ava whispered.

'Old enough to make you wish it stayed buried,' Isla said, scanning the perimeter with wary eyes.

That was when the silence broke.

A rustle, faint but sharp, from the trees. Too deliberate to be the wind.

Isla's hand shot up in warning. 'Movement,' she hissed. 'North ridge. Not local wildlife.'

Rafi tensed, his usual grin gone. 'Scouts?'

Dante's posture shifted instantly, every muscle coiled tight. 'Scouts,' he confirmed. 'Keep low. Eyes sharp.'

Ava's pulse spiked. 'Scouts for what? Who, '

'They hunt these islands,' Rafi cut in, voice pitched low. 'Men descended from Anderson's old crew. Smugglers. Wreck divers. Whatever they are now, they're feral, dangerous. They guard these islands like sacred ground, and they don't take kindly to strangers digging where they shouldn't.'

Isla's rifle was already up, barrel trained on the dark tangle of trees. 'They're not just guarding, Raf. They're following. Always following.'

The jungle erupted.

A blur of movement, shadows darting between the trees. The sharp twang of a bowstring. The hiss of something slicing past Ava's ear and thudding into the timber behind her.

Before she could process it, Dante was there.

One second he was a few paces ahead, the next his arm was around her waist, dragging her down and spinning her behind him in one seamless motion. The flash of steel as his cutlass left its sheath was blinding, a clean, terrifying arc of light.

A figure lunged from the undergrowth, all rage and sharp edges, but Dante met them mid-swing. The clash of steel rang out, brutal and final. The stranger crumpled at Dante's feet without a sound.

Ava's breath came in ragged gasps as Rafi swept the area, blade drawn, scanning every shadow.

'They'll regroup,' Isla said, voice cold and steady. 'Scouts don't work alone.'

Dante turned, grey eyes locking on Ava's with searing intensity. His hand tightened on her wrist, grounding her, commanding her attention.

'You see now?' His voice was a harsh whisper, rough with something she couldn't name. 'This isn't a story, Ava. This is blood and bone, and men who'd slit your throat before you could scream. You wanted adventure. This is it.'

Ava swallowed hard, her pulse hammering. Every rational part of her screamed to go, to run, to put as much distance as possible between herself and this cursed island.

But she held his gaze, chin lifting in defiance.

'I'm not leaving,' she said, her voice steady even as fear clawed at her ribs. 'Not until I know the truth.'

Something flickered in his expression, not softness, but something sharper. More dangerous.

'Then don't fall behind, Red,' he murmured, releasing her wrist.

By the time they made it back to the beach, the sun was dipping toward the horizon, staining the waves in bruised purples and molten gold. Ava stood in the shallows, the water tugging at her boots as she tried to steady her breath, the boat rocking gently nearby.

Behind her, Dante lingered at the treeline, staring back at the jungle, at the shadows that had swallowed the island whole.

'Anderson,' he muttered, almost to himself, the words carried on the sea breeze. 'What the hell were you hiding here?'

Chapter Six:
Blood in the Water

The ocean was black glass beneath a bruised sky.

Ava sat at the rail, arms braced against the cool, salt-streaked wood as the ship cut a clean line through the waves. The island they'd left behind was only a dark smudge on the horizon now, swallowed by night, but it clung to her anyway: in the taste of copper at the back of her throat, in the way the hairs along her arms still stood on end.

She could still hear it, the sharp hiss of arrows slicing through the air, the guttural sound the man made when Dante's blade found him.

And the way Dante had looked at her.

Not like she was fragile. But like she was his to keep.

A shiver ran down her spine, sharp and involuntary, and she tightened her grip on the rail until her knuckles blanched.

"You're shaking, Red."

The voice came from behind her, deep and smooth, carrying that strange blend of accents: the hard edges of South Africa tangled with something warmer, older, from the Caribbean.

She turned slowly, finding him there in the shadows.

Dante.

Leaning against the mast like the ship itself bent to him, coat half open, dark hair wild from the sea wind. His cutlass still hung at his hip, the blade freshly cleaned but the hilt slick with salt and something darker.

Ava straightened, forcing steel into her spine. "I'm not."

A ghost of a smile curved his mouth, humourless. "Lie better."

Her jaw tightened. She hated that he could read her so easily, like her fear was painted across her skin in colours she couldn't see.

"I didn't ask to be dragged into this," she said finally, voice sharp as the night air. "I just wanted, "

"What?" he cut in, stepping forward, shadows spilling off him like ink. "A holiday? A nice little island-hopping tour? That island isn't some postcard, Red. It's a graveyard. And you'd be bones in the sand right now if I hadn't, "

"If you hadn't what?" She bit the words out before she could stop herself, heat flaring in her chest. "If you hadn't swooped in like some… some saviour with a sword? You think I don't know how dangerous this is?"

For a beat, silence stretched between them, taut as a line ready to snap.

Then Dante moved closer, slow and deliberate, until there was barely a foot of space between them. His presence swallowed her whole; the scent of salt and smoke clung to him, the sharp edge of leather and steel.

"You don't," he said, voice low, dangerous. "You've read stories. Anderson the pirate, the outlaw who took what he wanted and burned the rest. But stories don't bleed. They don't scream. That island does."

Her breath hitched, but she didn't look away. Couldn't.

"I grew up on those stories," she whispered, forcing steadiness into her voice. "My dad… he used to tell them around the fire, out at Lucky Bay. Said Anderson wasn't just a pirate, said he was a ghost. A man who never stopped running, even after the sea swallowed him."

Something flickered in Dante's eyes at that, a flash of interest, sharp and sudden.

"Your father," he said. "He told you about Anderson?"

"Everyone in Esperance knows," Ava said, shrugging like her pulse wasn't hammering. "He was… larger than life. Dangerous. Clever. Untouchable. Kids grow up daring each other to swim to the reefs where his ships ran aground. Half the fishermen out here still swear they've seen him, standing on the rocks at dusk, watching the water."

A long, quiet pause followed. Only the groan of the ship and the steady hiss of the waves filled the space between them.

Finally, Dante spoke, his voice softer now, stripped of that sharp, commanding edge.

"And what do you believe, Red?"

The question stole her breath.

She looked down at the ink-black water below, at the way the moon fractured across the surface like broken glass.

"I think," she said slowly, "that a man doesn't just disappear. Not someone like him. I think… whatever happened to Anderson, it's still out here. Waiting."

Dante studied her, something unreadable in his expression, and for a moment she felt pinned in place by the weight of his gaze.

Then he stepped back, the moment shattering like glass underfoot.

"Get below," he said, voice clipped again. "Storm's picking up."

Ava hesitated. "What about you?"

"I don't sleep when the sea looks like this," he muttered, turning toward the helm. "Neither should you."

Sleep didn't come easy.

When it did, it dragged her down fast and hard, into something hot and vivid and impossible to shake.

She dreamed of fire, of a storm bleeding across the horizon, of the ship pitching beneath her feet as hands like iron gripped her waist.

Dante.

Close enough to feel the heat of him, to hear the low rumble of his voice against her ear, words she couldn't make out, drowned by the roar of the sea.

His mouth on hers, fierce, claiming, before the dream snapped like a taut rope, jerking her awake.

Ava sat bolt upright in the narrow bunk, breath ragged, skin damp with sweat that had nothing to do with the heavy air below deck.

Above, the ship groaned. The storm Dante had warned about had come fast, battering the hull with sheets of rain that sounded like gunfire.

She shoved the blanket off and climbed to her feet, bare toes curling against the slick wood as she made her way up the narrow steps.

The deck was chaos.

Rain slashed sideways, cold and sharp, and the wind howled like a living thing, tearing at the sails. The crew moved like shadows, slick and sure, tying lines and shouting orders Ava couldn't hear over the deafening roar.

And there, at the helm, was Dante.

One hand braced on the wheel, the other gripping the rail, coat plastered to his broad shoulders by the rain. His face was a mask of focus, sharp and unyielding, eyes like storm glass.

Ava hesitated at the top of the steps, heart pounding. Something about him in that moment, wild and commanding, every muscle coiled like a predator ready to strike, stole the words from her throat.

He turned, as if sensing her, and for the briefest moment their eyes locked.

Something passed between them.

Something she didn't have a name for.

The deck tilted hard, and Ava stumbled, slamming her shoulder into the mast. The sting of it barely registered over the fury of the storm. Lightning split across the horizon, throwing everything into stark relief, the twisted ropes, the chaos of the crew, and Dante, immovable at the wheel, every line of his body tense with control.

A wave crashed over the deck, drenching her, stealing her breath.

"What the hell are you doing up here?" Dante's voice cut through the wind, sharp and commanding.

Ava blinked through the rain, coughing, her hair plastered to her face. "I, I couldn't stay below. I thought, "

"You thought what?" He turned the wheel sharply, muscles straining, bringing the bow around into the swell. "That this was some kind of game? You'll get yourself killed, Red."

His eyes, black in the stormlight, alive with something fierce and electric, pinned her where she stood. For a second, it wasn't fear in her chest, but something wilder, sharper.

The ship lurched again, ropes snapping like whips. Dante barked an order in a language she didn't recognise, his accent thickening with urgency, the sound of it dark and rough and grounding.

Then, just as suddenly, the storm shifted.

Not gone, the rain still lashed, the wind still howled, but the worst of it eased, the waves no longer clawing as hard at the hull.

Dante eased his grip on the wheel, jaw set tight as he scanned the horizon.

"Get below," he said again, quieter this time.

But Ava didn't move.

Instead, she stepped closer, the space between them humming like a live wire.

"Why Anderson?" she asked, voice shaking but steady enough to carry. "Why risk all of this, your ship, your life, for a dead man?"

For a long moment, Dante didn't speak. Rain dripped steadily from the rigging, the storm whining through the ropes.

Finally, he turned to her, eyes narrowing.

"You wouldn't understand."

"Then make me," Ava shot back, surprising herself. "Because right now, all I see is some arrogant pirate chasing a ghost."

His jaw tightened, and for a moment she thought he might turn away. But then something in him shifted, like a lock giving way, and his voice, when it came, was quieter. Darker.

"Anderson wasn't just a man," Dante said. "He was a map. Every reef, every current, every hidden cut of water in these islands, he knew them. Better than anyone alive. And he didn't just take gold. He buried it. Hoards of it. Enough to buy kings."

Ava swallowed, her heartbeat pounding.

"And you think finding his body will… what? Lead you to it?"

Dante's gaze locked onto hers. "I don't think. I know. His men hid him when he died. Buried him deep. You find the bones, you find the truth."

A chill prickled along her spine.

"They say," she murmured, "no one knows how he died. My dad said there were theories. That maybe one of his own men killed him. Or that the women, the ones he took, rose up. Shot him in his sleep and dumped him overboard."

Dante's expression didn't shift. "They're not just stories."

"You've seen something," Ava whispered.

He didn't answer at first. When he did, his voice was lower, reluctant.

"The Scouts," he said.

Ava frowned. "Scouts?"

"Not men. Not ghosts. Something in between." His eyes, so steady moments ago, went distant. "They watch the islands. They were his once. Part of his crew. Or what's left of them. When you get too close, they come. Always just out of reach. Always waiting."

A shudder ran through her.

"And you're… not afraid of that?" she asked, though her voice trembled.

His mouth twisted, not quite a smile.

"Fear keeps you alive out here," Dante said. "But it doesn't stop me."

Ava stared at him, breath catching. For the first time, she saw it, the obsession simmering beneath every word.

Whatever drove Dante wasn't gold. It was something deeper.

Something dangerous.

The ship lurched, and Dante's hand shot out, gripping her wrist, steadying her. The heat of his touch burned even through the cold night.

"Get below, Red," he said, low and rough. "Before you drown."

Below deck, the storm's roar dulled to a heavy growl, but Ava's pulse wouldn't settle. She sat on the narrow bunk, clothes still damp, the ghost of his hand burning on her skin.

Outside, the sea raged.

Inside, she did too.

Because for the first time, she didn't know if the greater danger was out in the black water, or above deck, wearing a devil's grin and a South African-Caribbean accent.

Chapter Seven:
The Island of Whispers

The sea calmed as dawn broke.

The storm had left the world raw and hushed, as if the ocean itself were holding its breath. Ava climbed up onto the deck, her boots still damp from the night before, her hair in a loose, salty tangle.

The crew moved in sharp, silent motions, checking ropes, repairing lines, adjusting the sails to the light morning wind. No one seemed inclined to speak, not to her, not to each other.

Except Isla.

"You look like hell," the woman said from the bow, a smirk tugging at the corner of her mouth as she coiled rope with neat, practised hands.

Ava blinked, momentarily startled. "Thanks. You always this charming before breakfast?"

Isla snorted, tossing her a skin of water. "Before, during, and after. Hydrate. Storm nights like that, you're lucky you didn't crack your skull."

Ava caught the skin and drank deeply, her throat still raw from salt spray and fear. "Lucky," she muttered.

Isla arched a brow, sharp eyes glinting like obsidian. "You survived Dante's temper, the Scouts didn't show, and you still have all your fingers. That counts as lucky out here."

Ava hesitated. "The Scouts… are they real? Or just some legend to keep people away from the islands?"

Isla's expression didn't change, but something in her gaze sharpened. "Legends start somewhere. You'll see."

By mid-morning, the archipelago loomed on the horizon, jagged black cliffs rising from the turquoise sea, the edges bleached white where waves crashed in eternal rhythm.

Ava leaned against the rail, staring as the island grew closer. It didn't look like much from a distance, just another dot of rock and sand, but as the ship cut through the shallows, she felt it.

A hum in the air.

A weight pressing down on her skin.

"First landfall," Dante said from behind her, his voice a low rumble. She didn't have to turn to know he was watching her, she could feel it. "Stay close when we go ashore. And keep quiet."

"Why?" Ava asked, trying for nonchalance.

"Because this place doesn't like strangers."

She almost laughed, but stopped when she caught the hard line of his jaw, the intensity in his dark eyes. He wasn't joking.

The crew lowered a longboat, and Ava found herself sandwiched between Isla and Rafi as they rowed toward the island. The closer they got, the louder the hum grew in her bones, as if the island itself were alive and aware of their intrusion.

The longboat scraped the shallows. Salt water splashed up Ava's calves as she stumbled onto the wet sand, her boots sinking deep.

Every step inland was a step away from the world she knew, Esperance, her family, her friends.

And for the first time, the reality of her disappearance struck her like a punch to the gut.

No one knew where she was.

Back home, there'd be panic by now. Messages unanswered, calls going straight to voicemail. Posters, maybe, social media posts screaming for answers, her name trending in local groups.

Would they think she was dead?

A ghost swallowed by the southern sea?

A part of her wanted to scream, to demand a satellite phone, to call her sister or her father or anyone, just to say she was alive. But another part, darker, quieter, whispered something else.

What if you don't want to be found?

Because what waited for her back home? Dead-end jobs, familiar streets, the weight of being predictable, ordinary. Here, on this strange ship with a dangerous man and a crew of outlaws, she wasn't Ava-from-Esperance anymore. She was… something else. Someone else.

And God help her, the thought of disappearing completely didn't terrify her as much as it should have.

The island smelled of wet earth and decay. Trees twisted upward like gnarled fingers, their roots knotted deep into the sand. As they pushed inland, the noise of the ocean faded, replaced by an eerie, thick silence.

"This is… unsettling," Ava whispered.

"Welcome to the Recherche," Isla said with a dark little smile. "Every island has a story. None of them end well."

They hiked for nearly an hour before the first signs of human presence appeared, a broken camp: long-rotted canvas, rusted cutlery, a half-buried chest eaten away by time and salt.

Rafi crouched by the remnants, brushing sand off a warped, waterlogged journal. He turned a page carefully, his sharp eyes scanning the faded ink.

"Dates line up," he murmured, more to Dante than to anyone else. "Mid-1800s. Could've been one of Anderson's camps."

Ava knelt beside him, heart thrumming. "So… what happened here?"

"Take your pick," Isla said, arms crossed as her gaze swept the tree line. "Shot by his own men, taken by the Scouts, starved. Depends which story you believe."

Ava frowned. "And you? What do *you* believe?"

Isla met her eyes, and for a moment, Ava saw something unguarded there, something sharp-edged and old.

"I believe," Isla said quietly, "that men like Anderson never die easy. And that whatever killed him didn't stay buried."

The deeper they went, the worse it became. Bones lay scattered along the path like breadcrumbs, some bleached white with age, others cracked and sharp-edged, as if gnawed.

By the time they reached the clearing, Ava's skin was slick with cold sweat.

"Here," Dante said, crouching beside a shallow depression in the earth. The sand there was darker, still damp despite years of sun and wind. He brushed it aside with calloused hands until something hard caught the light, a long, narrow shard of bone.

The air shifted, heavy and electric, and the hum Ava had felt since landfall rose to a piercing note behind her eyes.

"Jesus," she breathed, stepping closer despite herself. "That's, that's human, isn't it?"

"Femur," Dante said flatly, holding it up. "Male. Big. Strong." His gaze lifted to hers, unreadable. "Could be him."

Silence fell over the clearing. Even the wind seemed to hold its breath.

Then, somewhere beyond the trees, a whisper.

Ava froze. "Did you hear that?"

Isla's hand clamped around her arm. "Don't look," she hissed.

"What?"

"Scouts," Isla said, voice low and tight. "They don't like being seen. And if they think you're hunting too close, "

A rustle cut through the underbrush. Something moved just beyond sight, deliberate and unhurried.

"Back to the boat," Dante snapped, all command now. "Move."

The trek back blurred, panic, snapping branches, the thud of Ava's heartbeat. She stumbled once, but Isla hauled her upright without a word.

"Keep moving," Isla muttered, sharp but steady. "Don't listen. Don't look."

By the time they reached the shore, Ava's legs were shaking, her lungs burning. They shoved the longboat into the surf, every moment stretched thin.

Only once they were back aboard the ship, the island shrinking to a dark smear behind them, did Ava finally exhale.

That night, Ava sat on the deck with Isla, a bottle of rum between them, stars sharp above. The adrenaline had faded, but the hum, that strange, low thrum, lingered in her bones.

"You get used to it," Isla said, breaking the silence.

Ava snorted softly. "I doubt that."

Isla smirked but didn't argue. She took a swig and passed the bottle across. "You held your own today. Not bad for someone who still thinks sunscreen is enough out here."

Ava gave a small smile. "Thanks for… you know. Back there. I would've, "

"Gone under," Isla finished. She shrugged, casual, but her gaze was steady, warmer than Ava expected. "Don't mention it. We look out for each other. Whether we want to or not."

For the first time since being dragged aboard the Night Reaver, Ava felt something new. Not safety, she wasn't foolish, but connection.

"Isla?" she asked quietly.

"Yeah?"

"Why are you here? On this ship. With him."

Isla was silent a long moment. Then, lightly, but not lightly at all:

"Because sometimes you find someone whose madness matches yours. And because leaving isn't always an option."

Their eyes met in the dim, shifting lamplight, and Ava understood, not everything, but enough. Enough to know that whatever bound Isla to Dante was not simple.

And maybe, just maybe, she was beginning to feel that same pull.

Ava stared out toward the horizon, fingers curled around the bottle. Somewhere out there, Esperance was still moving on, her name whispered, her face on screens.

Maybe tomorrow she'd send a message.

Maybe tomorrow she'd tell them she was alive.

But tonight, with the ship humming beneath her and stars glittering overhead, the thought of staying a ghost, unseen, unclaimed, unbound, felt almost intoxicating.

Chapter Eight:
Ghosts and Fire

The ship cut through the water with brutal efficiency, slicing across the dark stretch of the Southern Ocean like a predator. The archipelago was far behind them now, just a distant shadow swallowed by the horizon.

But the island's hum, that strange, oppressive weight, still lingered in Ava's chest. It pulsed beneath her skin, quickening every time Dante's eyes landed on her.

She hated that.

And she hated that she didn't truly hate it.

Ava paced the deck, restless. The night air was sharp, biting through the thin cotton of her borrowed shirt. Below, the crew murmured and laughed, their voices carried up on the breeze.

She wanted to scream. To cry. To leap overboard and swim back to shore until her body gave out.

Instead, she stood there, a ghost in the dark, invisible to the world she'd left behind.

"You keep walking like that," Dante's voice rumbled from the shadows, "you'll wear a hole clean through my deck."

Ava spun, pulse spiking. He leaned against the mast like he'd been born there, arms folded across his broad chest, shirt loose enough to show the hard cut of muscle, tattoos inked dark against sun-browned skin.

"Maybe that's the idea," she snapped. "Make a hole, sink the damn ship, and swim home."

His brow twitched, amused. "You wouldn't make it a mile in those waters, Red. Sharks would have you before sunrise."

"Stop calling me that," she hissed.

She moved toward him before she could think, anger buzzing hot under her skin. "Maybe I wouldn't be fighting you if you'd just, just let me go."

Dante pushed off the mast in one slow, deliberate step, closing the space between them. The deck tilted under her feet, or maybe it was just the way his presence swallowed everything around her.

"Why did your father talk about Anderson?" he asked, voice low, dangerous. "You know stories, yes? About his treasure. His death."

Ava swallowed, throat tight. His breath was warm, edged with rum. "Why does it matter?"

"Because you know something," Dante growled, accent thickening, rough. "Your old man told you things. Things I need."

Her temper flared, bright and reckless. "You think you can scare it out of me? What if I don't know anything? What if I just, "

"Liar," he said, soft but lethal. "You've got that look in your eyes, Ava. You've had it since the day you stepped on my deck. You know him. Or you think you do."

Her hands curled into fists. "I know the stories. My dad talked about Anderson like he was some kind of legend. Like a man who couldn't be killed. I grew up on those stories. He said Anderson didn't die. That he'd come back."

Dante's jaw tightened, something unreadable flickering there. "And what do you believe?"

Ava's chest rose and fell in sharp, angry breaths. "I don't know what I believe anymore. I just know I want to go home."

The silence that followed was sharp enough to cut.

Dante stepped closer, close enough that the heat of him curled around her, dizzying, wrong, intoxicating. "You're not ready for home," he said softly, voice a low, dangerous promise. "Not yet."

Her pulse thundered, wild and traitorous. She hated him. She wanted him. And she hated herself for wanting him.

Later, when the ship went quiet, Ava found herself below deck, tucked in a narrow corner of the galley where Isla sat cross-legged on a barrel, a cigarette hanging from her lips.

"You look like you just survived a hurricane," Isla said dryly, exhaling smoke.

Ava dropped into the space opposite her, pulling her knees to her chest. "Feels like it."

Isla watched her for a moment, then flicked the cigarette into an empty bottle and leaned back. "Don't let him get under your skin. That's how he wins."

Ava let out a rough huff of a laugh. "A little late for that."

Isla tilted her head, eyes softening, only slightly. "He's not easy. Never has been. But… he's not the villain you think, either."

Ava blinked. "You're defending him now?"

"Not defending," Isla said quietly. "Explaining." She hesitated. "Dante saved me. I was ten. Storm wrecked our ship off Geraldton. Everyone went under."

Ava stilled. "Everyone?"

"Everyone," Isla repeated, voice flat with old grief. "I clung to a barrel for two days. Thought I'd die. Then he shows up, twenty, half mad, and pulls me out. Didn't even ask my name. Just… kept me. Raised me like blood."

The weight of it settled between them.

Ava whispered, "I'm sorry."

Isla shrugged one shoulder. "Don't be. I owe him my life. Doesn't mean I don't want to strangle him most days." She smiled, small, sharp, real. "You'll figure that out, too."

Silence folded around them again, softer this time. The ship creaked. The ocean breathed.

For the first time since being dragged aboard, Ava didn't feel entirely alone.

Above them, the sea stretched black and endless.

And somewhere at the helm, Dante stood in the dark, staring toward the horizon like he could outrun the ghosts chasing him.

Chapter Nine:
The Island of Bones

The morning broke grey and sharp, the horizon painted in bruised steel. The ship cut through the surf like a blade, and Ava stood near the rail, clutching   white.

Salt spray stung her cheeks. The wind lashed her hair into wild tangles, the chill biting through the thin fabric of her borrowed shirt. She should have been used to the ocean by now, the relentless thrum of the waves, the ceaseless creak of wood and rope, but today felt different.

Darker.

Below deck, Isla hummed an old song, the kind that spoke of ghosts and sailors swallowed by storms. And at the helm, Dante barked clipped orders in that rough, rolling accent of his, Caribbean melody laced with South African steel.

The air thrummed with tension.

They were heading for Bones Island.

"Why do they call it that?" Ava asked, her voice small against the roar of the wind.

Isla leaned against the rail beside her, a quiet shadow, her dark braid whipping behind her. "Because it's where men go to die," she said simply, eyes fixed on the jagged silhouette rising from the waves. "Currents are brutal. Reefs sharp enough to gut a ship in seconds.

And…" She hesitated, lips pressing tight. "And because it's where they say Anderson's trail went cold."

Ava's chest tightened. Her father's stories came rushing back, tales whispered by the firelight of an infamous outlaw, a man who defied every storm, every rival. A man who vanished without a trace.

"Do you think he died there?" she asked quietly.

Isla's gaze flicked to her, unreadable. "Depends on which story you believe."

By midmorning, the island loomed close enough that Ava could see the pale slash of sand, the black teeth of rock that framed its shores, and the dense tangle of forest crouched beyond.

"Drop anchor!" Dante's voice cut through the salt-heavy air.

Ava turned just as his gaze found hers. Something sharp flickered in those dark eyes, challenge, warning, heat, before he vaulted down to the deck with a fluid grace that made her pulse hitch.

"Gear up," he ordered. "We go ashore in five."

She wanted to argue, to demand why she needed to go, but the words tangled and died on her tongue when he stepped closer.

"You want freedom?" he said, voice pitched low so only she could hear. "Then earn it. Learn what we're chasing."

The skiff hit the shore hard, skidding up on the wet sand with a jolt that rattled her teeth. Ava scrambled out, boots sinking into the cold grit, heart hammering as she took in the bleak sprawl of the island.

Silence. Not the soft quiet of dawn, but the heavy, suffocating kind that pressed in from all sides.

"This place gives me the creeps," Isla muttered, pulling her rifle over her shoulder as she scanned the tree line. "Scouts don't even come here unless they're desperate."

"Scouts?" Ava asked, breathless as she tried to keep up while Dante led them inland, his long strides eating the distance.

Isla shot her a look. "Salvagers. Mercenaries. Treasure hunters. They smell blood in the water, and they don't care who they cut to get what they want."

A chill prickled down Ava's spine.

The forest swallowed them whole within minutes, the air thick and wet, the smell of rot clinging to every breath. Branches snagged her hair, her clothes. The ground sucked at her boots, each step an effort.

She trailed behind Dante, trying not to stare at the way his shoulders moved beneath his shirt, the easy, lethal way he carried himself, like the jungle itself bent to his will.

And then the ground shifted.

Bones.

Ava froze, breath stuttering as her gaze locked onto the pale curve of a skull half-buried in the damp earth, moss creeping over its hollow sockets. Around it, ribs and vertebrae jutted like broken teeth, tangled in the roots of an ancient tree.

Her stomach lurched.

"Storm wreck," Dante said without looking back, voice flat. "Bodies get dragged in, trapped in the tide pools. Happens every season."

But the way his shoulders tightened told her this wasn't just another wreck.

They found the first marker at the edge of a lagoon, a crude wooden post carved with symbols Ava didn't recognise, half-swallowed by the tide.

Dante crouched, brushing sand away with careful fingers, the sharp planes of his face caught in shadow.

"What is it?" she asked, stepping closer despite herself.

"Coordinates," he murmured, eyes narrowing. "Old ones. He left a trail."

Ava's heart tripped. "Anderson?"

He looked up at her then, dark eyes catching hers, unreadable, intense. "Aye. Always two steps ahead. Even in death."

The words sent a shiver through her, sharp and cold.

By the time they reached the cliffs on the far side of the island, the sky had begun to change, clouds rolling in thick and low. The air tasted of rain and electricity.

Dante halted, one arm shooting out to stop her as a sharp crack split the silence.

Gunfire.

Ava froze, pulse roaring in her ears.

"Scouts," Isla hissed, dropping low, her rifle sliding into her hands like an extension of her arm. "They're already here."

Dante swore under his breath, eyes scanning the cliffs above. "Stay behind me," he snapped at Ava, voice like steel.

"No," she whispered, panic clawing up her throat. "I, I can't just, "

"Stay." The command cracked through her like a whip, leaving no room for argument.

The next few minutes blurred, shouting, the distant pound of boots, the sting of fear slicing through every nerve.

Ava ducked behind a jagged outcrop of rock, heart hammering as bullets tore through the sand near her feet.

And then Dante was there, a wall of heat and muscle shielding her as he dragged her closer to cover, his breath harsh against her ear.

"You want to die, Red?" he growled, voice rough, dangerous. "Because that's how you die."

Her fingers curled into the front of his shirt, clutching tight. "I didn't ask for this," she choked.

His gaze locked on hers, something fierce and unspoken burning there. "Neither did I," he said softly, almost broken.

The moment snapped when Isla shouted from above, voice sharp and urgent: "Clear, for now. Let's move."

They reached the cave just as the sky split open, rain lashing down in blinding sheets. Inside, it was dark and damp, the air thick with salt and old secrets.

At the far end, buried beneath a collapse of stone, something glinted.

Dante moved first, muscles coiling as he heaved rocks aside with practiced ease.

When the last stone fell away, Ava stepped forward, breath catching.

It wasn't a treasure chest.

It was a journal.

Leather cracked and blackened with age, edges curled from water and time.

Dante lifted it with a reverence she'd never seen from him, hands careful, almost trembling.

"His," he whispered, voice hoarse. "Anderson's."

Ava swallowed hard, heart pounding as she stepped closer. She could see the faded ink, the sprawl of letters in a hand both wild and deliberate.

"What does it say?" she asked, voice barely more than a breath.

Dante didn't answer. He just stared at the pages, expression a storm she couldn't read.

By the time they made it back to the skiff, the rain had turned the sea into a roiling fury.

Ava sat silent as they fought their way back to the ship, the journal clutched tight in Dante's grip, the weight of what they'd found pressing on all of them.

Isla sat beside her, quiet, damp hair plastered to her skin. After a moment, she reached out, fingers brushing Ava's.

"You okay?" she asked softly.

Ava hesitated, then nodded. "Yeah. I just… I don't know what I'm doing here."

Isla's gaze softened. "None of us did, at first. But you'll figure it out. Or you won't. Either way… you're not alone anymore."

Ava swallowed, something warm and fragile unfurling in her chest.

Not alone.

When the ship finally steadied, Dante disappeared below deck with the journal, leaving Ava restless and aching in ways she couldn't name.

She found herself standing at the bow hours later, wind sharp against her damp skin, the horizon stretching endless and black ahead.

Somewhere in the dark, the storm still raged.

And deep in her bones, she knew this was only the beginning.

Chapter Ten:
The Calm Before

The ship was quiet in the strange, eerie way it always was after a discovery.

The journal sat on the chart table in Dante's quarters, bound in cracked leather, its brass clasp dulled by salt and time. Ava had seen him take it below deck the moment they had returned from the island, his hand gripping it so tightly his knuckles had turned white, and he had not let it out of his sight since.

Now, he was locked away. And the ship, despite the steady hum of the ocean and the gentle creak of timber, felt… still. Far too still.

Ava sat cross-legged on her bunk, twisting a piece of her damp hair between her fingers. Every time she closed her eyes, she saw it: Dante crouched in that cavern, his torchlight spilling over the blackened bones, the carved symbols, and that cursed journal. She remembered the way his jaw had clenched, his shoulders rigid, his eyes unreadable as he slipped the book into his coat and walked out without a word.

And then, nothing. Silence.

For hours.

It was not just the mystery of what was in the journal that made her uneasy. It was the way he had looked at her before disappearing into his quarters, like she was a storm forming, one he was not sure he could face.

She hated the way her chest tightened at the memory.

"Staring at the wall isn't gonna get you answers," Isla said from the doorway, leaning against the frame with her arms crossed. She wore her usual smirk, but there was an edge to it tonight, sharp and protective.

Ava glanced up, startled. "I wasn't..."

"You were," Isla interrupted, stepping into the room. She dropped onto the opposite bunk, dark hair spilling across her shoulder. "Don't bother lying. You've got that look, the one that says you're desperate to know what's in that bloody book but too stubborn to ask."

Ava pressed her lips together, unwilling to admit Isla was right.

"It's not just that," she muttered.

"No?" Isla raised a brow. "Then what? Frightened of him?"

Ava hesitated, her voice barely a whisper. "Maybe I should be."

Isla watched her for a long moment, the playfulness fading from her face. Then she reached into her pocket and pulled out a small knife, rolling it between her fingers as though it were part of her hand.

"When I was ten," she began, her voice softer now, "my father worked cargo routes out of Fremantle. Storm season hit, and the ship went down halfway to Singapore. I don't remember the wave that took us under, just… the cold. Hours of it. Days, maybe. I woke up clinging to a barrel, and there he was."

Ava's chest tightened as Isla nodded toward the deck, toward where Dante was, always, somewhere above or below, a shadow that seemed ever-present.

"He didn't have to haul me out," Isla said. "Didn't have to bring me aboard, feed me, teach me how to survive this life. But he did. And not for the first time." She fixed Ava with a steady look. "That man's got his demons, Red. But when it comes to his crew, to his people, he'd bleed for them."

Ava swallowed hard. "And you trust him."

"With my life," Isla said simply. Then her mouth tilted into a wry half-smile. "Doesn't mean he won't drive you mad in the process."

The words lingered long after Isla left, and Ava found herself restless. She could not sit still, could not ignore the pulse of tension humming beneath her skin.

It was late when she finally gathered the nerve to find him.

The ship rocked gently in the dark, moonlight glinting off the black water as she padded barefoot across the deck. Every step brought her closer to that heavy oak door, to the muted glow of lantern light spilling out beneath it.

She hesitated, fingers hovering near the latch, before knocking once.

Silence.

Then: "Come in."

His voice was low, rough, carrying that edge that always seemed to wrap around her spine.

Ava pushed the door open.

Dante was at the table, sleeves rolled up, a tumbler of dark liquor at his elbow. The journal lay open before him, its pages splayed like an old wound. He did not look up as she stepped inside, did not move as the door clicked shut behind her.

"I need to know what's in it," she said, her voice steady despite the thunder in her chest.

"You don't," he replied, turning a page without meeting her eyes.

Her hands curled into fists at her sides. "You think you can keep me in the dark? You dragged me into this, Dante. You kidnapped me, remember? And now you want me to just sit here and pretend I don't care why you're chasing the ghost of a dead pirate?"

That got his attention. Slowly, he lifted his head, his eyes dark and sharp and burning.

"You think this is a game, Red?" His voice was quiet, dangerous. "That this is some grand adventure where you get to play tourist while I do the hard work?"

Her pulse spiked, heat rising through her veins. "I think," she shot back, "that you're so obsessed with him you can't see what it's doing to you. To everyone on this ship. And maybe you're scared that if you actually tell me the truth, you'll have to admit you're not in control."

For a moment, the only sound in the room was the steady creak of the ship and the distant rush of the waves.

Then he moved.

One moment he was across the room, the next he was there, close enough that the space between them felt dangerously small. His presence was overwhelming, salt and sun and danger, the heat of him brushing against her skin like a spark waiting to catch.

"Careful, Red," he murmured, his voice a low rumble that wrapped around her like smoke. "You don't know what you're asking for."

Her breath caught, her heart hammering against her ribs. "Then tell me," she whispered, her voice trembling with something she did not want to name.

For a heartbeat, he just stared at her, unreadable. Then, with a sharp curse, he turned away, shoving the journal closed with a snap that cracked through the room.

"Not tonight," he said, rough and final. "Go. Before you learn what it means to burn."

Ava did not sleep.

She lay awake in the dark, the hum of the ocean loud in her ears, Dante's words and the heat in his eyes tangling through her thoughts. She hated the way he got under her skin, the way her body betrayed her even as her mind begged her to keep her distance.

By dawn, she had almost convinced herself to let it go.

Almost.

The day passed in a blur of chores and tense glances. Dante was a ghost on deck, barking orders without ever looking her way. Isla, as perceptive as ever, drifted close when she could, offering quiet reassurances Ava did not know how to accept.

By dusk, the horizon was bleeding gold and violet, the air heavy with salt and secrets.

Ava found herself leaning against the rail, staring out at the endless stretch of water. Somewhere out there, beyond the rolling waves and shifting tides, was the world she had left behind, her family, her friends, the life she once knew.

She wondered if they thought she was dead.

The thought sent a strange, electric thrill through her.

To them, she was a ghost now, gone without a trace, swallowed by the sea.

And maybe, a small, reckless part of her whispered, maybe she preferred it that way.

That night, as the crew settled into uneasy sleep, Ava lingered near the stern, the hum of the ship beneath her feet. From below deck, she caught the low murmur of voices, Dante's, rough and clipped, and Isla's softer, steadier.

"…not like the others," Dante was saying. "…won't let her end up the same."

"Then stop pushing her," Isla replied, her voice quiet but fierce. "She's not the enemy, Dante."

A pause. Then a sound, frustration or maybe pain.

"She's a liability," Dante muttered. "And if she stays..."

"You'll protect her," Isla cut in, firm and certain.

The conversation faded into murmurs, but Ava stayed frozen where she was, her pulse thundering in her ears.

Back in her bunk, the ship swaying gently beneath her, Ava stared up at the low ceiling, sleep a distant impossibility.

Because whatever secrets were locked inside that journal, whatever path Dante was dragging them toward, one thing was certain.

There was no turning back now.

Not for her.

Not for any of them.

Chapter Eleven:
Ghosts in Ink

The ship rocked gently in the quiet before dawn, that hour when the sea held its breath, waiting for the sun. Ava couldn't sleep. She had tried lying still, tried willing her body into rest, but every time she closed her eyes, her mind knotted itself in questions, about the journal, about Dante, about why she hadn't fought harder to go home.

The deck smelled of salt and smoke. Someone, Dante, perhaps, had been up here through the night, pacing. She imagined him leaning over the rail, jaw tight, the way he always was when his thoughts turned dark. She'd learned enough about him now to know when his silence meant danger.

By the time she worked up the nerve to go below, her hands trembled.

The captain's quarters were dim, lit only by the swaying glow of a single lantern. Dante sat at the desk, broad shoulders bent, the journal open in front of him like a wound. He didn't look up when she entered, just turned the page slowly, carefully, as if afraid the old ink might disappear at his touch.

"You shouldn't be here," he said, voice quiet but not sharp. More weary than anything else.

"You keep saying that," Ava murmured, her gaze fixed on the journal. "And yet you never stop me."

Silence settled for a moment. The ship creaked around them. The lantern flickered, shadows crawling across the walls.

Finally, Dante looked up. His dark eyes caught the light, unreadable.

"This isn't a game, Ava," he said, voice edged with something heavier than warning. "Anderson… he wasn't the kind of man you grew up hearing stories about. Not really."

"Then tell me," she said, stepping closer. "Show me."

Something in him shifted, subtle, almost unseen, but enough. He turned the journal, its cracked leather cover facing her, and slid it across the desk.

Her breath hitched. Slowly, she lowered herself into the chair opposite him and traced her fingertips over the brittle pages. The ink had bled and faded in places, but the words… the words were alive.

November, 1834

Seas scream louder tonight. Men whisper of scouts in the water.

They think I don't hear.

Gold sleeps where they cannot see it, buried deep as bone.

No map, only the tide and my memory.

They'd kill me for it. Maybe they already plan to.

The archipelago keeps its dead.

And if I die here, so will the truth.

A chill ran down Ava's spine as her eyes skimmed the page, the words scratching at something deep in her chest.

"Gold," she whispered. "From the rush."

Dante nodded, leaning back, his expression unreadable. "He moved more than rum and women. Mainland miners trusted him with shipments, trades. Some say he smuggled half a fortune through these islands during the height of the gold rush, gold that never made it back to shore."

"And you think…" Ava's voice faltered. "You think it's still out there?"

"I know it is." His gaze locked onto hers, unwavering. "Anderson didn't trust anyone. He wouldn't have left it behind unless he meant to return."

Further in, the journal darkened. The handwriting grew jagged, almost frantic.

Sophie Jane

March, 1835

They follow me. Scouts in the dark, eyes like glass.

The tide changes. The wind dies.

I hear their teeth at night.

No sleep. No trust. Only the gold and the girl.

The girl knows too much.

Ava swallowed hard, throat tight. "The girl?"

Dante's jaw flexed. "No one knows. A lover. A captive. Maybe just another name in a story that twisted over time."

She stared at the page, heart pounding. Scouts in the dark. Eyes like glass.

She'd heard murmurs from the crew, shadows watching the ship from a distance, that prickling sensation on the back of the neck in the dead of night. And now, seeing it written in Anderson's hand, she felt the words sink into her bones like cold water.

"What happened to him?" she asked softly. "To Black Jack."

Dante leaned forward, elbows on his knees. "No one knows for certain. Some say his crew turned on him, shot him over the gold. Others think the women he kept… the ones who worked his camps… finally slit his throat and dumped his body overboard. And then there are the old tales, that the Scouts dragged him into the deep, that they marked him for death."

"And you believe…?"

His mouth lifted, not quite a smile. "I believe Anderson was too smart to die easy. But no man cheats the sea forever."

The ship rocked hard, and the lantern swung wildly, casting arcs of light across the cabin. For a heartbeat, Ava swore the shadows in the corners deepened, leaning closer.

Her hands trembled as she turned another page. The ink here was smeared, the lines fragmented.

50

Beneath Southern Stars

April, 1835

The barrel girl clings to my shadow.

She thinks I can save her.

No one is safe.

Not here.

Not where the tide bleeds red.

She snapped the book shut, heart thundering. The room felt too tight, the air too heavy.

"What aren't you telling me, Dante?"

He studied her for a long moment, gaze sharp and unflinching. "You want the truth? The gold, the journal, none of it matters if you don't make it through this. The Scouts don't leave witnesses."

Her breath caught. "So what? I'm just... what? Another burden to you?"

His jaw clenched, something raw flickering in his eyes. "You're not a burden, Ava," he said quietly. "But you're not ready for what's coming."

For a long moment, neither of them spoke.

The ship groaned under the weight of the tide. Footsteps thudded above, Isla's, likely, but Ava couldn't move, couldn't look away.

Later, on deck, the horizon burned with the orange of an approaching storm. Ava stood by the railing, the salt wind stinging her cheeks, the journal heavy in her hands. Isla drifted over silently, like she always did, her dark hair whipping across her face.

"You've been reading," Isla said softly.

Ava nodded. "It's... a lot."

Isla's mouth curved into something almost like a smile. "It always is."

Silence settled between them, the easy kind. Then Isla spoke again, voice low and steady.

"Black Jack wasn't just a man, Ava. He was a storm. People think he died because someone got greedy, or because the Scouts dragged him under. But sometimes…" She paused, eyes faraway. "Sometimes I think the sea just takes what it wants."

Ava turned to her. "And you? What does it want from you?"

Isla's gaze lingered on the water, her voice barely a whisper. "It already took everything."

The words hung heavy, as dark as the sky above them, and Ava realized, not for the first time, how deeply this ship, this strange, cursed world, had carved into these people. Into Dante. Into Isla.

And, though she wished it weren't true, into her.

By nightfall, the storm was close enough that the air seemed to hum, waves slapping harder against the hull. Ava lay awake in her berth, the journal pressed to her chest, the words burned into her mind.

The archipelago keeps its dead.

She didn't know if that was a warning, or a promise.

Chapter Twelve:
The Storm Breaks

The storm swept in hard and fast.

By nightfall, the ship pitched violently, waves clawing at its sides as if the ocean wanted to rip it apart. Ava clung to the railing, hair plastered to her face, the taste of salt sharp on her tongue. Every gust of wind stole her breath; every crack of thunder rattled her bones.

"Get below!" Isla's voice cut through the roar, sharp with authority. She darted across the slick deck like a shadow, bracing a rope with one arm while signalling Ava toward the stairs.

But Ava didn't move. Something wild had wormed its way into her chest, fear, yes, but mixed with something hotter, fiercer. Her pulse hammered in her ears, impossible to ignore.

Then Dante was there. A dark silhouette in the chaos, his broad frame cleaving through the storm like it bent around him. His hand shot out, gripping her arm in an iron hold, spinning her toward the companionway.

"What the hell are you doing out here?" His voice was ragged, scraped raw. "You'll get yourself killed."

She jerked her arm free, breathless, furious. "I'm not some porcelain doll, Dante. I don't need you..."

The ship lurched violently. Her feet slipped, the world tilting, and for a heartbeat, nothing existed but the shrieking wind and the terrifying sensation of falling.

Then his arms wrapped around her, strong, unyielding, pulling her hard against the heat of his chest.

Her heart stuttered, then raced.

"Why don't you ever listen?" His face was close now, too close, dark eyes glittering with something wild in the dim light. Rain streamed down his sharp cheekbones, dripping from his jaw, but his grip didn't loosen. "Out here, you don't get second chances, Ava."

She glared up at him, trembling but unbroken. "Then stop treating me like cargo and tell me why I'm really here."

For a moment, the storm itself seemed to pause. The space between them crackled, alive, like the charged air before lightning strikes.

"You want the truth?" His voice was low, dangerous. "You're here because I can't let you go."

The words hit her harder than the waves hammering the ship. She blinked, caught between fury and something far more perilous, the white-hot spark that had been simmering between them since the day he dragged her aboard.

Before she could reply, the boat lurched again, hurling them both against the mast. She gasped, her palms braced against his chest, feeling the solid, unyielding strength beneath her fingertips. His breath came fast, rough, his eyes locked on hers.

Then Dante kissed her.

It wasn't soft or hesitant. It was fierce, consuming, the collision of two storms too strong to avoid. She tasted salt and rain and something unmistakably him as his hand cupped the back of her neck, pulling her closer, anchoring her even as the world spun wildly around them.

Ava made a sound, half fury, half need, and gripped his soaked shirt, dragging him closer. The wind howled, the ship groaned, and for one reckless moment, there was nothing but heat and the dizzying rush of wanting.

When they pulled apart, both of them were breathless, the storm roaring louder than ever around them.

"This is insane," she whispered, but her voice shook, betraying her.

"Everything about you is insane," Dante growled, his forehead resting against hers, his hands firm on her waist as if letting go wasn't possible. "And I can't stop."

Neither of them moved. Neither of them blinked. The world could have ended right there, swallowed by the sea, and she wasn't sure she would have cared.

By the time they stumbled below deck, the storm had eased, but the electricity between them hadn't.

The corridor was dim, lantern light swaying with the soft roll of the sea. Ava could still feel the pulse of the storm under her skin, could still taste him, and it left her shaken. Breathless.

She should have gone to her bunk. Should have locked herself in and put up a wall high enough to keep him out.

But when his hand brushed hers in the narrow passageway, a deliberate, fleeting touch, every thought scattered.

She stopped. So did he.

The space between them was razor thin, dangerous.

"You should stay away from me," Dante said, voice low and strained.

"Then why aren't you moving?" Her whisper came out sharper than intended, betraying the tremor in her chest.

For a long moment, neither of them moved. The lantern light caught on his jaw, on the dangerous angles of his face, and Ava's heart pounded hard enough to hurt.

Then, slowly and deliberately, Dante stepped closer, until her back brushed the wall and the heat of him caged her in.

His fingers found her wrist, just a ghost of a touch, then traced upward, slow, until they rested at the curve of her shoulder.

"This," he said softly, almost brokenly, "is a mistake."

"Then stop," Ava breathed, though her body betrayed her, leaning into his touch.

But he didn't stop.

The kiss that followed was nothing like the one on deck. This one was quieter, slower, but no less consuming. His hands framed her face, calloused thumbs brushing her cheeks, and when she kissed him back, something inside her snapped.

There was no room for thought, no space for reason. Only the two of them, tangled in the dim light and the hum of the ship, caught in something too big to name and too dangerous to ignore.

His hand slid to the small of her back, pulling her flush against him, and a shiver ran up her spine. Ava clung to him, nails digging into his shoulders, the heat of him searing through the thin barrier of her clothes.

Somewhere in her mind, a warning flickered, don't want this, don't want him, don't get dragged under, but it drowned beneath the weight of everything else. The crash of waves, the taste of him, the sharp, breathless ache of needing.

The air inside was heavy, thick with the scent of rain, salt, and something else. Something electric.

He didn't speak at first. Just stood there, towering, water dripping from his hair, his chest rising and falling like a man fighting for control.

"You should hate me," he said finally, voice low and rough. "After everything, you should hate me."

"Maybe I do," she shot back, though her voice trembled.

His eyes darkened, but he didn't move. Didn't speak. Just studied her, as if deciding whether to push her away or pull her closer.

Then she moved, or maybe they both did. She wasn't sure who crossed the distance, only that his mouth was on hers again, harder, hungrier, like the storm had never ended.

Later, tangled in the dim light, Ava stared at the ceiling, her pulse still erratic. Dante sat on the edge of the bed, head bowed, hands clasped, tension running sharp through his shoulders.

"Why do you look like you regret it?" she asked quietly.

His head lifted, slow, deliberate. "Because I told myself I wouldn't do this. Wouldn't drag you deeper into something you don't understand."

She sat up, clutching the thin sheet to her chest. "Maybe I want to understand."

His jaw tightened, but he didn't answer. Outside, the storm had passed, the ship swaying gently in the calm after chaos. But inside, the air still thrummed with the unspoken, with everything they had unleashed but hadn't named.

The morning sun rose slow and low, burning gold into the pale sky, turning the sea into molten fire. Ava sat cross-legged on the deck, her hands wrapped around a chipped enamel mug of lukewarm coffee. The storm from the night before had passed, but its echo lingered in the salt crust on her skin, the ache in her muscles, and the wildfire of emotion still racing through her chest.

She shouldn't have thought about him. Shouldn't have remembered the heat of his hands, the reckless press of his body, the impossible closeness of his mouth against hers in the dark below deck. But she couldn't help it. And now, as she stared at the calm horizon, the quiet felt almost worse. It left her alone with thoughts she couldn't silence.

Isla slid onto the deck beside her, bare feet warm against the wood, her presence steadying. "You're far too quiet," she said, nudging Ava's shoulder. Her voice was gentle, teasing.

Ava forced a smile. "Just thinking. Nothing important."

Isla narrowed her eyes. "Right. Thinking. You've got that look, like you're deciding whether to throw someone overboard or jump in yourself. Maybe both."

Ava let out a shaky chuckle. "Maybe both."

"You need a distraction," Isla said, leaning back against the railing. "Come help me check the ropes and sails. Better than sitting here letting the sun cook your brain."

Grudgingly, Ava rose, letting Isla lead her through the familiar rhythms of the ship. As they worked, she found herself noticing things she hadn't before: the way Isla moved, precise and lithe; the small laughter that escaped when Ava missed a knot; the way her eyes softened when she gave instruction rather than scolding.

Later, as the sun climbed higher, a flicker on the horizon caught Ava's eye. A small vessel, distant but unmistakable, slicing cleanly through the calm sea. She squinted, heart pounding.

"Isla," she whispered, pointing.

The older girl followed her gaze, lips tightening. "Scouts. They're close. Too close."

Ava's stomach dropped. For the first time since boarding the ship, she felt the deep, familiar fear of being hunted, the stories of Black Jack Anderson's death had always whispered through her childhood. She felt it now, as real as the wind biting at her cheeks.

Dante appeared without a sound, standing behind them like a shadow. His eyes fixed on the distant ship, dark and unreadable. His hand brushed hers, a brief, possessive touch that set her nerves alight.

"They're nothing we can't handle," he said, voice steady. Then, softer, almost to himself, "But you need to stay close."

Ava's pulse spiked at the heat in his tone. Protective, yes, but something else too. Something personal. Something dangerous.

The days that followed blurred, softened around the edges by stolen glances and touches that lingered longer than they should have. Ava told herself it meant nothing, that it was adrenaline or proximity, a way to anchor herself in a shifting world.

But every time his hand brushed hers, every time his gaze met hers across the deck, she knew she was lying.

One evening, when the sea was calm and the crew quiet, Dante found her leaning against the railing, staring at the endless horizon. The sky was streaked with orange and violet, the water a mirror of fire.

"You're thinking too loud," he said, his voice softer now, lacking its usual harshness.

Ava shot him a look. "And what am I thinking?"

"That you don't know where you belong anymore."

She didn't answer, but the silence between them was answer enough.

Dante stepped closer, close enough that his presence wrapped around her like warmth. "You're not the same girl I dragged onto this ship."

"And whose fault is that?" she asked, though her voice lacked venom. His mouth curved, but it wasn't a smile. "Mine."

Later, when the world went quiet and only the sound of the sea filled the spaces between them, Ava let herself wonder what it would mean to stay, to choose this life, this chaos. To choose him.

But for every spark of longing, there was fear, sharp and undeniable. Fear of losing herself. Fear of what lay waiting in the shadows of these islands, of what the journal had whispered in its fragmented, haunting script.
And fear, most of all, of what it would mean when Dante finally told her the truth about why she was here.

Chapter Thirteen:
The Edge of the Sea

Hours later, the tension of the sea and the distant threat of the Scouts pressed heavily on Ava's chest. The ship rocked gently underfoot, a deceptive calm after the storm had ripped through the night. The horizon was an endless silver ribbon, sunlight reflecting off the waves in sparkling shards, yet the calm felt hollow. Every creak of timber, every whisper of wind through the rigging made her pulse quicken, a constant reminder that danger lingered just beyond sight.

Ava couldn't shake the feeling that her world had shifted the moment she crossed the threshold into Dante's life. That night below deck had left an imprint she couldn't erase, a mixture of fear, heat and desire humming in her veins with every heartbeat.

She found herself slipping away, almost unconsciously, to Dante's cabin. The deck was quiet, the crew scattered in small groups or below, checking damage from the previous storm. Ava moved like a shadow, her bare feet silent against the worn planks. She felt the weight of the journal in her bag, the brittle leather almost humming with secrets, calling to her in a voice she couldn't ignore.

The cabin was dark, the lantern swinging gently, casting flickering shadows across walls lined with maps and charts. Ava placed the journal on the chart table, the familiar smell of old leather and ink filling her senses, grounding her in a world suddenly alive with the unknown.

She opened it slowly, careful not to tear the fragile parchment. The ink had bled, but the words were still legible, sharp and haunting, as though Black Jack Anderson's voice reached through decades to speak directly to her.

"The sea will take everything. Yet she gives back what you least expect, and it will cost you more than blood."

A shiver ran down her spine. The words felt like more than a warning, more than a promise. They felt directed at her alone.

Footsteps approached, soft against the wooden deck. Ava froze. Dante leaned in the doorway, arms crossed, watching her, dark eyes unreadable. The tension between them was palpable, charged with something electric that made her stomach twist.

"You read it," he said simply.

"I… I wanted to," Ava admitted, her voice low. "It feels like… like it's calling to me."

He stepped into the room, closer than necessary, and the air between them thickened. Every small movement seemed magnified, the shift of his weight, the curve of his shoulder, the dark curl of hair clinging to damp skin. "You know more than you think," he said quietly, voice rough, almost intimate. "About the ocean, about survival. Your father left traces of it in you, in your instincts, your recklessness. You'll help me navigate this."

Ava's eyes widened. "You need me?"

He didn't answer at first, simply studied her, intensity burning in his gaze. Finally, he said, voice low and urgent, "Not just want, Ava. I need you. If we're going to survive the Scouts, find what Anderson left behind… I need your knowledge, your courage, and your mind."

Her stomach twisted at his admission. Not the kind of confession she expected. Not lust or longing, though that simmered between them too. This was deeper. Dangerous. Real.

"I don't know if I can do that," she whispered, heart hammering. "I barely know you."

"You know more than you think," he repeated, stepping closer. The proximity made her knees weak, the heat between them unmistakable. "And you're learning fast. That's why I brought you here. Not just to keep you alive, but to survive."

Ava's fingers traced the journal's pages, seeking comfort in the brittle words. She could feel him behind her, the heat of his body so close it left her trembling. She wanted to turn, wanted to lean into the danger, but caution held her still.

Dante reached for the journal, brushing her fingers. "Every page tells a story," he murmured. "And some of those stories aren't finished. Some of them… are ours to write."

The words sent a shiver through her. And in that instant, Ava realised the truth: Dante didn't just want her. He couldn't do this without her.

Outside, the sea rolled quietly, deceptive in its calm. The Scouts could strike at any moment. The horizon held danger, hidden and patient.

Inside, the two of them remained still in the small cabin, the weight of the past, the journal, and the unspoken fire between them binding them tighter than either would admit.

"Dante," Ava whispered, voice trembling, "what if I fail?"

His gaze softened slightly, though it stayed intense. "You won't," he said. "Not because you're fearless, but because you've survived worse than you realise. And because you're not alone. Not here, not on this ship."

She swallowed hard. There was comfort in his words, but fear too. Fear that once she let herself belong to this world, to him, there would be no going back.

The day passed in a blur of movement. They inspected sails, checked lines, and Isla watched the horizon, sharp and alert. Ava kept herself busy, running her hands over knots, memorising the ship's every creak and sway. But every task dragged her thoughts back to Dante, his words, his gaze, the unspoken heat between them.

As night fell, the first whisper of a distant ship cut across the water. A dark silhouette, faint against the fading light. Ava's heart froze.

"Scouts," Isla muttered, her voice tight. She pointed at the horizon. "Too close."

Dante appeared behind Ava in a heartbeat, eyes narrowing. "Stay calm," he ordered, though the edge in his tone betrayed the danger. He moved between Ava and the rail, a living shield, his presence both terrifying and protective.

Ava felt a jolt of conflicting emotion, fear, yes, but also an undeniable pull towards him. He needed her, and for the first time, she felt she couldn't run from that reality.

The hours stretched, tense and taut. The Scouts did not approach aggressively, only skirting at a distance, testing the waters. Dante's vigilance never faltered, his hands moving constantly, adjusting sails, scanning the horizon. He was all control, all focus, yet when he glanced at her, that same dark heat flickered, dangerous and nearly impossible to resist.

Later, when the deck quieted and night settled fully, Ava slipped once more into Dante's cabin, journal in hand. The lantern's glow cast long shadows, making the space feel smaller, more intimate.

She opened it to a page she had skipped earlier. The words seemed to writhe beneath her gaze:

"Trust is a currency the sea exacts heavily. Those who betray it pay with blood, those who cherish it survive, but not unscathed. The girl knows the ocean. The boy needs her. Both are bound by what they cannot yet see."

Ava's pulse hammered. The journal felt prophetic, almost alive.

Dante appeared behind her, close enough that his presence warmed her skin. "I wasn't lying," he said softly. "Your father knew more than he let on. More than anyone suspected. That knowledge is in your blood, in your instincts. And it's why I can't do this without you."

Ava gripped the journal. "So you need me… not just because you want me?"

He didn't answer at once. Instead, he stepped closer, closing the small gap between them. "Not just want. Need," he murmured. His voice was low, urgent, a growl that made her shiver. "You keep the ship alive. You keep us alive. And…" His hand brushed hers, lingering.

"...you keep me from going under, from losing focus. From losing everything."

Ava's chest tightened. Every instinct screamed danger, yet something darker urged her closer. She wanted him, wanted the chaos, the thrill of losing control.

The journal lay on the table, a fragile thread tying past to present. And Ava understood then that her life, her heart, and the truth of the ocean were bound to Dante's now.

Outside, the sea remained calm, but Ava knew better. Calm never lasted. The Scouts waited, the horizon held secrets, and the storm would return, both in the water and between them.

And Ava, for all her fear and confusion, knew she would face it. She had no choice. She belonged to this world now. To him. To the chase.

Chapter Fourteen:
The Scouts Strike

The horizon cracked with movement before Ava even realised it.

Isla's sharp voice cut through the night air: "There! Three points off the starboard bow!"

Ava squinted, heart hammering. Small silhouettes against the silver sheen of the sea, distant at first, but fast, precise and unrelenting. The Scouts. They weren't coming to parley. They were coming to kill, to capture, to take what Dante had spent years hiding.

Dante appeared beside her, dark eyes narrowing, jaw tight. The familiar heat and intensity radiating off him did little to calm her nerves. If anything, it amplified the fire coiling in her chest, equal parts fear and something dangerously unnameable.

"They're testing us," he said, voice low, almost a growl. "But they're too close to be ignored. Ready yourself."

Ava's fingers clenched around the railing, knuckles white. "I… I don't know what to do."

"You already know more than you think," Dante said, his hand brushing hers, a fleeting, possessive touch that made her pulse spike. "Stay sharp. Watch the sails. Watch me. Trust your instincts."

The Scouts were closing faster, slicing through the calm sea like knives. Ava's breath caught as their small craft lifted briefly on a wave, the moonlight glinting off its sharp edges. Her mind flashed to the journal, to Black Jack Anderson's words, and a flicker of resolve ignited.

"I've got this," she whispered to herself. And somehow, to him.

The first volley came without warning. A shout, the clatter of weapons, and a harpoon skimming dangerously close to the deck. Dante barked orders, swift and precise, and Ava moved almost instinctively, adjusting sails, tightening ropes and holding her ground as the ship lurched beneath her. The Scouts were skilled, faster, smaller, more agile than Dante had warned, and the night became a blur of motion, shadow and salt.

"Keep the lines taut!" Dante yelled, eyes scanning, calculating. He was everywhere at once, a master of the chaos, and yet Ava saw something in his movements, restraint, calculation, a fierce protective edge she had never felt before.

"You can't let them board us," he muttered, almost to himself, then, sharper: "Ava, the main sheet! Pull it now!"

Her muscles screamed, her fingers cut against the ropes, but she obeyed. The ship heaved, groaned and tipped violently to port as a Scout's boat skittered dangerously close. Heart racing, she felt the heat of Dante behind her, guiding, correcting, his presence like a shield.

Then it happened, one of the Scouts' harpoons grazed the rail, splintering the wood near her feet. Ava stumbled, yelping, and Dante's arms were around her in a heartbeat, pressing her against his chest. The scent of rain and leather and something wild and intoxicating surrounded her.

"Stay with me!" he shouted over the chaos.

She did. She had to.

Hours seemed to collapse into minutes. The battle was a storm unto itself, the Scouts darting and striking, Dante countering, Isla keeping watch and executing orders like a shadow, and Ava finding herself moving with a confidence she hadn't known she possessed. Every instinct her father had drilled into her, every story she had clung to about Anderson, every fear and thrill collided into action.

And all the while, Dante was there. Always close. Always protective. Always that impossible mix of danger and magnetism.

During a brief lull, they found themselves pressed together in the cramped corner of the deck, eyes locked. The adrenaline still surged, the danger still loomed, but in that heartbeat of stillness, Dante's hand brushed against hers, deliberate and lingering, and the tension between them ignited into something that made Ava's knees weak.

"You did well," he said, voice low and dangerous. His dark eyes held hers, unblinking, and for a moment, the Scouts, the danger, the world beyond the ship ceased to exist. "I can't do this without you."

Ava's chest heaved, the journal's words echoing in her mind. Not just want. Need. The truth of it pressed down on her like a wave, impossible to ignore.

"I'm not afraid," she whispered, though the tremor in her voice betrayed her. "Not of you. Not of this."

Dante's gaze softened, almost, before hardening again as a shout cut through the night. The Scouts were regrouping, circling, testing their defences.

"Then let's finish this," he said, voice edged with both heat and steel. "Together."

The next wave of attacks was a blur. Ava's hands moved over the ropes and sails with uncanny precision, her instincts guiding the ship as Dante countered the Scouts' every manoeuvre. She felt alive in a way that terrified and exhilarated her. Every command Dante barked, every calculated risk he took, drew her closer, not just physically, but emotionally, in a way that made her heart ache.

At one point, the Scouts attempted to board. Ava's breath caught as one of them swung over the rail, but Dante intercepted him with a brutal force that sent the man sprawling back into the water. He barely glanced at Ava, but she could feel his presence, the raw energy of him, surrounding her, anchoring her even in the chaos.

"You're extraordinary," he muttered when the Scout sank beneath the waves. "Do you know that?"

Ava's pulse thundered. "You're dangerous," she shot back, though the words carried something else, recognition, admission, desire.

Dante's lips twitched into a shadow of a grin, and for a moment, danger, passion and adrenaline collided into a heady, intoxicating storm.

Hours later, after the Scouts had finally retreated beyond the horizon, Ava and Dante collapsed onto the deck, drenched in sweat and salt, hearts hammering. The sea was calm again, deceptively serene, as though it had swallowed the night's violence whole.

Ava's gaze wandered to the journal, resting in her lap. The words seemed more urgent now:

"The girl knows the ocean. The boy needs her. Both are bound by what they cannot yet see."

She shivered, realising the truth in them. Not just about the sea, or the Scouts, or even Black Jack Anderson. About them.

Dante sat close, close enough that the heat of him radiated into her, and yet distant in a way that made her ache. "You did more than survive tonight," he said quietly, voice rough. "You were necessary. Without you…" His words trailed off, but the intensity in his gaze filled the space.

Ava's chest tightened. She wanted to reach for him, to let herself give in to the fire between them, but caution held her back, that razor-sharp awareness that their bond, however magnetic, was forged in danger and secrecy.

Yet, even as she wrestled with the fear and desire, she felt a profound shift. She wasn't just a passenger. She was part of this ship, part of Dante's life, part of the story unfolding across the dangerous, haunted waters of the Recherche Archipelago.

The night stretched on. Ava stayed near the rail, hands still trembling from the adrenaline. Dante was nearby, patrolling the deck, ever-watchful, and yet his eyes found hers often, burning with a mixture of need and caution, want and restraint.

"You understand now," he said finally, voice low, almost a growl. "You're part of this. Not just because I need you, but because the sea, the Scouts, Anderson's legacy, none of it works without you. None of it."

Ava swallowed, chest tight with fear and something darker, fiercer. "I… I think I understand."

His hand brushed hers again, light but deliberate, and the simple contact sent a thrill racing through her. "Good," he murmured. "Because I can't let you go. Not now, not ever."

The Scouts had retreated for now, but Ava knew the calm was only temporary. Danger was never far. The ocean never rested. And neither would the obsession that bound her and Dante together, fast, fierce and utterly unstoppable.

Chapter Fifteen:
Fire on the Water

The night was thick with fog, heavy and choking, as the Tempest carved her path through the dark waters. Ava's muscles still ached from the previous encounter with the Scouts, but exhaustion was a luxury she couldn't afford. Her hands gripped the railing, knuckles white, eyes straining to pierce the grey haze. Every sound, a creak, a splash, a whisper of wind, set her pulse racing.

Dante moved along the deck like a shadow, silent and deadly, every step measured. Even in the fog, his presence was unmistakable, the heat radiating from him, the low hum of controlled tension. Ava couldn't stop stealing glances at him, her chest tightening at the mere sight.

"You're too close to the rail," Dante said, voice cutting through the fog. His hand brushed hers in a fleeting, almost casual touch, but it left her trembling. "Stay alert."

"I am," she murmured, though her voice betrayed the fire still burning in her chest.

He glanced at her, eyes narrowing, lips pressing into a thin line. "Not enough."

The Scouts struck without warning. Shadows moved on the water, fast and silent. One moment the sea was empty, the next, ropes and grapnels slashed across the deck as a small boat smashed into the Tempest's side. Ava's heart leapt into her throat.

"Boarders!" Dante roared, and in a heartbeat, he was between her and the rail, guiding her back, his hands firm and commanding. "Get down!"

Ava obeyed, ducking low as the first of the Scouts swung aboard. The clash of steel rang out, sparks flying as blades met. Isla moved like a ghost, fast and precise, taking down anyone who dared approach.

Dante's gaze flicked to her, and Ava felt it like a tether pulling her through chaos. "Stay close. Watch me."

She did, moving with him, reacting instinctively, her father's lessons and her own instincts blending seamlessly with Dante's commands. Every movement was a dance, fast, dangerous and thrilling.

A Scout lunged at Dante from behind. Ava froze for a split second, too long. He parried, but the man's blade grazed Dante's shoulder, tearing his shirt and drawing blood. Dante growled, spinning the attacker onto the deck and knocking him out with brutal precision.

Ava's heart raced as Dante turned to her, his dark eyes blazing. "You're reckless!" he snapped, though the heat in his gaze was impossible to ignore. "One wrong move—"

"I'm not afraid!" she shot back, heat and adrenaline coiling in her voice.

Dante's expression softened for the briefest moment, the anger and danger in his eyes giving way to something raw and magnetic. "You should be," he muttered, stepping closer, the faint smell of salt and iron filling her senses. "This is the sea, Ava. It doesn't forgive mistakes."

Her chest heaved, and the pull between them became impossible to ignore. Yet the fight wasn't over. Another Scout swung over the rail, and Dante intercepted him before Ava could react, forcing her back.

The battle on deck became a blur of movement. Blades clashed, ropes flew, and the ship lurched under the pressure. Ava's mind focused, almost eerily calm amid the chaos. Every instinct, every lesson from her father, every story of Black Jack Anderson guided her hands. She worked the rigging, dropped sails at the perfect moment, and even managed to throw a Scout off balance long enough for Dante to strike him down.

Then, disaster.

A Scout managed to grab her, pulling her toward the edge of the ship. Panic shot through her, sharp and sudden, as she struggled, nails digging into his arm.

"Let her go!" Dante bellowed, and in a terrifyingly fast motion, he swung a blade, cutting the attacker free just as Ava nearly tipped overboard. The man crashed into the water with a splash, leaving Ava trembling, soaked and breathless.

Dante's hands were on her immediately, gripping her shoulders, eyes blazing with a mixture of fury and something deeper. "Do you understand now?" he hissed. "Do you see why I need you here?"

Her chest heaved, the heat of him, the danger, the raw intensity almost too much to bear. "Yes," she whispered, voice trembling. "I understand."

For a long moment, they simply stood there, pressed close, the storm of adrenaline and fear leaving them raw and exposed. Dante's hands lingered at her waist, just enough to remind her of his presence and his desire without crossing a line.

"You saved yourself," he murmured, voice low and rough. "But more importantly… you saved me. Again."

Ava's fingers brushed his arm, tentative, and her heart pounded. "We saved each other," she said, though the words sounded hollow even to her. She wanted him desperately, and yet the fear of losing herself held her back.

Dante's gaze darkened, intensity coiling like a storm. "It's not just about survival," he said, voice husky. "It's about this… about us. You're part of this now, Ava. Not just the ship, not just the mission, but me."

Her breath caught, and for a second, the world narrowed to the space between them, heat, danger and an unspoken promise that neither could name.

The Scouts were gone for now, retreating into the night. The Tempest rocked gently, deceptively calm, the tension lingering like a shadow.

Ava sank to the deck, shaking, exhausted, but alive, and more aware than ever of the dangerous pull Dante had over her.

He knelt beside her, dark eyes softening just slightly. "You were incredible," he said, voice low, almost intimate. "I need you like this. Every day, every decision, every fight. Without you, none of this works."

Ava's chest tightened. Not just want. Need. Again, the truth struck her harder than any wave, any blade. She couldn't deny it. She wouldn't.

"I… I don't know what I am," she admitted, voice trembling. "But I know I can't stop being here. With you. On this ship."

Dante's lips brushed hers, quick, dangerous, a fleeting contact that sent sparks through her veins. "Good," he murmured. "Because I won't let you go. Not now, not ever."

The night stretched on, quiet for now, but Ava knew the calm was temporary. The Scouts would return. Danger lurked at every horizon, and the ocean itself was unpredictable.

Yet in that moment, beneath the moonlight and the quiet lapping of waves, Ava realised something terrifying and exhilarating. She was part of Dante's world, bound to him by danger, passion and the unrelenting pull of fate.

And she wouldn't have it any other way

Chapter Sixteen:
Aftermath and Secrets

The dawn was reluctant, pale and hesitant, spilling over the horizon in muted greys. The sea was deceptively calm, as if the night's violence had never touched it. Ava sat on the deck, knees pulled to her chest, fingers tracing the grains of wood as if they could anchor her to reality. Every creak of the ship, every whisper of wind, reminded her of what had happened.

The Scouts had retreated, but their presence lingered like a shadow over the Tempest. Ava's chest still ached from the adrenaline, from the fear, and from the awareness that Dante had risked himself, again, to protect her. She could still feel his hands on her, his heat pressed against her back, and a shiver ran through her.

Isla moved around the deck quietly, repairing damage from the boarding. The efficiency with which she worked, the quiet determination in her movements, reminded Ava why she trusted Isla implicitly. The older girl's calm amid chaos was an anchor, and yet even she couldn't erase the memory of what had almost happened.

Dante appeared then, as silent and imposing as ever. He didn't approach directly but stood a few feet away, dark eyes fixed on her. The tension between them, thick and almost unbearable last night, had softened slightly in the daylight, but the fire simmering beneath the surface remained.

"You're awake," he said, voice low and steady. "Good. I need you alert today. The Scouts aren't gone. Not really. They'll regroup."

Ava's pulse quickened. "I know. I can feel it."

He stepped closer, the air around him charged, and for a brief moment, she thought the world had narrowed to just them, the sound of the ship, and the threat still pressing from the horizon. "Last night," he murmured, almost reluctantly, "was more than survival. You were extraordinary. Every instinct, every move, it saved us."

Ava swallowed. "I couldn't have done it without you," she admitted, the words tasting strange but honest. Her heart ached with the need to bridge the unspoken between them.

Dante's gaze softened just slightly. He moved closer, and she could feel the warmth of his body, the rhythm of his breath, and the intensity of his presence pressing against her senses. "You don't understand," he said, voice rough and intimate. "It's not just about the Scouts. It's about what's coming. What we're chasing. The treasure, the truth of Black Jack Anderson. Without you, none of it works."

Her fingers brushed the edge of the journal at her side, a thin thread tying the past to the present. She traced the words again, the brittle paper almost alive beneath her touch. "The girl knows the ocean. The boy needs her. Both are bound by what they cannot yet see."

She shivered. Every line felt written for her, a warning, a guide, a prophecy. And the thought that Dante needed her for more than mere survival sent a shiver through her chest, dangerous and thrilling.

The morning passed in tense preparation. Sails were checked, ropes tightened, and Isla kept a vigilant eye on the horizon. Dante worked beside Ava, their movements coordinated, instinctively synchronised, yet every glance carried the weight of the night before.

"You're growing stronger," he said as she adjusted the main sheet. "Faster, sharper, more daring than I expected."

"I learned from the best," Ava shot back, heat and amusement flickering in her tone, though her pulse still raced. The memory of his hands on her, of his nearness in the dark, haunted her every motion.

His lips quirked, a shadow of a smile. "And yet," he said quietly, almost teasing, "you nearly got yourself killed."

"Nearly?" Ava challenged, heart hammering. "I thought it was pretty close to actually dead."

The faint laugh that escaped him was dark, dangerous and intimate. For a moment, the world felt lighter, though the danger lurking beyond the horizon was never far.

Later, as the ship drifted through calmer waters, Ava found herself again drawn to the journal. The pages were fragile, curling at the edges from salt and time, yet each word seemed to pulse with life. She turned to a passage she had skipped before:

"The ocean takes those who forget her lessons. Those who remember carve a path through her depths. Some paths are marked in blood, others in secrets. And the one who understands both survives."

Her breath caught. It was impossible to ignore the weight of the words, as though Black Jack Anderson had written them knowing that someone like her would read them decades later.

Dante appeared behind her without a sound. His gaze fell on the open page. "And there it is," he said, voice low, almost reverent. "The first clue. Anderson left more than treasure. He left warnings. Guides. For someone who could read them."

Ava met his eyes, understanding dawning. "And he meant me?"

Dante's expression softened just slightly, the tension in his jaw easing. "Yes. You. Your knowledge of the ocean, your instincts, your father's lessons, they were meant to prepare you for this. I need you, Ava. Not just to survive, but to find what he left behind."

The words sent a thrill and a fear coiling through her chest. She understood finally: her life had been steering her here long before she ever saw the Tempest.

Evening fell, painting the sky in deep purples and reds. The ship was quiet, the crew tending to repairs, the Scouts nowhere in sight for now. Ava and Dante found themselves on the deck, alone, the sea stretching endlessly around them.

The fire between them, simmering for days, now threatened to ignite fully. Dante stepped closer, eyes dark, unreadable yet impossibly intense. "I can't keep pretending," he said, voice low and urgent. "I want you here. Close. Always. Not just because I can't do this without you, but because I don't want to be without you."

Ava's pulse thundered. She wanted him, yes, but she also feared the consequences: the danger, the ship, the secrets, all of it. And yet, the need, the heat, the undeniable pull between them was impossible to deny.

"I don't know if I can—" she began, but he closed the space between them with a slow, deliberate movement.

"You can," he whispered. "And you will. Because you're mine now, and I won't let go."

The tension, the danger, the passion, everything collided into a single moment of awareness. Ava realised she didn't want to escape. Not from him. Not from this life. Not from the fire that had been ignited, dangerously, uncontrollably, between them.

Outside, the sea whispered secrets in the dark. The Scouts were still out there, patient and relentless. But inside that circle of moonlight on the deck, Dante and Ava stood together, bound by danger, desire and the unrelenting pull of fate.

The treasure, the journal, the past of Black Jack Anderson, all of it waited. And so did the next storm.

But Ava was ready. Because for the first time, she knew she wouldn't face it alone.

Chapter Seventeen:
Secrets on Middle Island

The longboat slid into the cove of Middle Island under a sky streaked with pink and gold. The morning fog still clung to the jagged cliffs, curling in wisps around the rocks like spirits guarding their secrets. Ava's pulse thrummed with anticipation and nerves; the island was small, isolated, but every inch of it felt charged with mystery.

"This is it," Dante said, voice low, almost reverent. He leaned against the railing, eyes scanning the treeline. "Middle Island. Somewhere in its heart, we'll find what Anderson left behind, or at least a clue to the next step."

Ava's fingers brushed the journal in her bag, its worn leather comforting under her touch. "And if it's dangerous?" she asked, voice tight. "I've survived Scouts, storms… what makes this any different?"

Dante's gaze softened, dark and dangerous, yet filled with a rare warmth. "Because we're together. And because the ocean doesn't give up her secrets easily. But you? You have the mind for it, the courage. And…" He stepped closer, heat radiating from him, "…I need you."

Ava's chest tightened at the words. The pull between them, simmering for days, felt impossible to resist. She forced herself to focus: adventure, danger, mystery, and the man beside her who had become as essential as air.

The crew anchored the ship, and Dante led Ava and Isla through dense undergrowth toward a cliffside trail that led inward. Middle Island was rugged, almost wild, the scent of salt and wet stone thick in the air. Birds called overhead, and distant waves crashed against hidden coves. Ava felt like she was walking through a place untouched by time, yet charged with the echoes of someone else's past.

"Keep your eyes open," Dante warned. "Anderson didn't leave this willingly. If he wanted us to find something, he hid it well. And there are hazards."

Isla fell into step beside Ava, her tone quieter now, more intimate. "The Scouts know these islands too. If they follow us, they won't hesitate. Stay close and keep alert."

Ava nodded, feeling the bond between herself and Isla deepen. They had begun to share glances, small smiles and quiet reassurances, a sister-like alliance that grounded her when the tension with Dante felt almost too much to bear.

They came to a series of jagged rocks forming a natural staircase into the island's interior. Here, Dante paused, pulling out a compass and map. "According to Anderson's notes," he murmured, "there should be a marker. Something subtle. Something only someone who knows what to look for would notice."

Ava's eyes flicked to the journal. She opened it, flipping carefully to a page marked by a fold, the ink faded but legible:

"The land holds what the sea could not. Follow the stone that points to the rising sun. There, the past waits for the brave."

She felt her pulse spike. "Stone that points to the rising sun?" she repeated.

Dante's eyes glinted. "You read that right. And we're going to find it. Together."

Hours passed as they climbed, clambering over rocks and winding through thick vegetation. The island seemed endless, every corner hiding shadows and secrets. Ava's legs ached, but she pushed on, driven by the journal and the growing knowledge that she was part of something far bigger than herself.

"Here," Dante finally said, pausing at a rocky outcrop. The sun had climbed higher, spilling warm light onto a formation of stones that jutted upward like the fingers of some ancient guardian. One of the stones leaned slightly east, casting a shadow directly at a hollow in the rock floor.

Ava's breath caught. "That's it. That has to be it."

Dante stepped closer, eyes dark and intense. "Anderson's clever. He wouldn't make it easy. Watch the ground. Watch the stones. There may be traps."

Isla grinned faintly. "Traps? Just like a real treasure hunt. I like this."

Ava rolled her eyes but couldn't hide the thrill rushing through her. Together, the three of them began examining the stones. Ava's hands brushed the edges, following grooves and indentations that hinted at purpose.

Then she found it, a small, almost imperceptible marking on the base of one stone, a symbol matching sketches in Anderson's journal. Her heart leapt. "This is it," she whispered.

Dante's gaze lingered on her, a flash of pride and something darker in his eyes. "You've got the eyes for this," he murmured, almost as if confessing a secret.

Ava's pulse thundered in her ears. "I… I just read the journal," she admitted, heat rising in her cheeks. "It guided me."

Dante's hand brushed hers in a fleeting, deliberate touch, sending a thrill through her. "You guided yourself," he said softly. "And now we see the first step of Anderson's secret."

They descended into the hollow revealed by the shadow, finding a hidden cavity etched into the rock. Inside lay small wooden chests, covered in dust and lichen. Ava's fingers trembled as she brushed away the debris, revealing a collection of maps, notes and artifacts, evidence of Black Jack Anderson's journeys and the treasure he had hidden across the archipelago.

"This… this is incredible," she breathed, scanning the maps, the coordinates, the meticulous notes. "It's more than gold. He documented the islands, hidden coves, secret passages. This could change everything we know about his routes."

Dante stepped closer, shoulder brushing hers, the heat between them undeniable. "And now," he said, voice low and intimate, "we follow it. Together."

Ava felt the pull, magnetic and irresistible. The danger, the secrets, the treasure and Dante himself, everything intertwined. She wanted him, yes, but she also wanted the hunt, the mystery, the thrill of being part of something larger than herself.

The island held its secrets tightly, the sea whispered outside, and the shadow of the Scouts still loomed, patient, watching, waiting.

But Ava and Dante were no longer just survivors. They were hunters, partners, and something more, tangled in fire, desire and destiny.

And on Middle Island, as the sun climbed higher, the first real threads of Black Jack Anderson's mystery began to unravel, and Ava knew that every step forward would bring danger, heat and revelation in equal measure.

By nightfall, the island was cloaked in indigo. The fire snapped and hissed in the cradle of stone, its glow painting the faces of the crew in gold and smoke. Isla leaned back on her elbows, eyes reflecting the flames, while Rafi rummaged through one of the smaller chests they had dragged up from the hollow.

"Look at this," he muttered, holding up a small, corroded compass. "Needle's busted, but the casing's pearl. Could fetch a fortune back in Perth."

Isla snorted softly. "You'd sell your soul if it shone bright enough."

"Depends who's buyin'," he shot back, grinning.

Ava smiled faintly, though her gaze was fixed on the spread of relics laid before them — cracked bottles, rusted tools, scraps of parchment sealed with wax. Each artifact felt alive, humming with stories they weren't meant to find. She traced one of the maps with her fingertips, the ink faint but legible.

Dante crouched opposite her, studying the drawings in silence. The firelight danced along his jaw, catching on the faint scar near his temple. He hadn't said much since the discovery, but Ava could feel the restlessness in him, a current running deep beneath the calm.

"What do you make of it?" she asked quietly.

He lifted his gaze, and the flicker of the fire turned his eyes to molten gold. "Anderson wasn't mapping trade routes," he said. "He was drawing a trail. For her. The coordinates follow no logic — they're personal."

"For Elara," she whispered.

He nodded once. "A man like him doesn't bury gold for greed. He buries it for love."

Isla yawned loudly, rolling onto her side. "Romantic, for a pirate," she said, already drifting toward sleep.

Rafi followed soon after, mumbling something about standing watch and then promptly collapsing beside the embers.

When their breathing settled into the rhythm of the waves, Dante stood and extended a hand. "Come with me."

Ava hesitated. "Where?"

"Up the ridge," he said. "There's a cave marked on one of the maps. I want to see it before dawn."

The climb was steep, the air damp and thick with the scent of salt and earth. When they reached the mouth of the cave, the firelight from their torch spilled across the walls, illuminating carvings — spirals, handprints, and the faint outline of a symbol Ava recognised from Anderson's journal.

"The same mark," she breathed.

Dante's hand brushed her shoulder as he stepped past. "He came here," he murmured. "Maybe this is where he said goodbye."

The walls shimmered faintly with mineral veins that caught the light like stars trapped in stone. The air was cooler here, quieter, as though the island itself was holding its breath.

"He loved her," Ava said softly, running her fingers over the carvings. "You can feel it. Even after all this time."

Dante turned toward her, his voice low. "Maybe love's the only thing that survives a man like him."

Ava looked up, and in the silence that followed, the tension between them stretched thin as glass. She could hear his breathing, steady but uneven, and see the struggle written across his face, the same battle she felt inside herself.

He reached out, his fingers ghosting over her wrist, tracing the pulse there. "You should've stayed on the ship," he murmured.

"And missed this?" she whispered. "Not a chance."

When he kissed her, it wasn't careful. It was hungry, desperate, the kind of kiss born from danger, discovery, and all the things neither of them could admit aloud. Her hands tangled in his shirt, pulling him closer until the cave seemed to pulse with their heat.

The taste of him was salt and smoke. The air between them trembled with want and warning.

When they broke apart, breathless, Dante rested his forehead against hers. "You make me forget what I came here for," he whispered.

"Maybe that's the point," she said.

For a moment, they stood there, two souls bound by the same storm, before the world found them again.

By dawn, the fire at camp had burned to embers. The wind had shifted, sharp and cool, carrying the distant scent of rain. Isla was already awake, standing at the ridge's edge, spyglass raised.

"Trouble," she said as Dante and Ava approached. Her voice was flat. "Scouts. Four boats, maybe five. South of the reef."

Rafi cursed under his breath, already packing the scattered relics back into the chests.

Ava's heart pounded. "How long?"

"An hour, maybe less," Isla replied. "They're moving fast."

Dante's jaw tightened. "We take what we can and move back to The Reaver. Now."

The sea below was darkening, the horizon bruised with storm clouds. Ava glanced back once, toward the hollow, the cave, the pieces of Anderson's life they'd barely begun to understand, then to Dante. His expression was iron, but his eyes still carried the shadow of the night before.

The fire, the touch, the words they hadn't said, all of it hung between them as heavy as the coming storm.

As they gathered the artifacts and made for the beach, Ava couldn't help but think that the real treasure wasn't what they'd found, but what they were about to lose.

Chapter Eighteen:
The Map of Bones

Gray light spilled over the deck of the Tempest as dawn rose sluggishly through mist. The sea shimmered like beaten pewter, calm yet deceptive, a stillness that never lasted long in these waters. Ava stood by the rail, the leather-bound journal open in her hands, the salt-warped pages whispering secrets in the wind.

Dante was below deck, charting their course toward the next set of coordinates carved into Anderson's notes. Isla was somewhere near the bow, checking damage from the previous night's fight. For once, Ava was alone, or nearly so.

The ocean hummed beneath her, a vibration she could feel in her bones.

She turned the journal to a section she hadn't dared open before. The ink had bled and blurred from salt, but the words were still there, ghostly and uneven, as if written by trembling hands.

"King Sound, 1836.

She told me the sea would take everything if I didn't return to her. I laughed. Fool that I was.

Now the sound carries her name. The tide sings it when the moon is high. I have left her behind once. I will not do it again.

If I fall, if I vanish, she will come back for what was always hers."

Ava's pulse quickened. She traced the faint signature at the bottom —

J. Anderson.

It felt like the words were meant for her, whispered across time. She will come back for what was always hers.

Her father had said something once, half a story, half a warning, about a woman lost to the tides near King Sound. A legend of a love cursed by the ocean's jealousy. Ava had thought it was just a tale for sailors. Now, she wasn't so sure.

"Reading without me?" Dante's voice broke her trance. He approached silently, his boots soft on the deck, his tone caught somewhere between curiosity and concern. His shirt was open at the throat, salt-streaked and stained from the last battle, but his eyes were as dark and unreadable as the sea.

Ava snapped the journal shut, but too late. He'd seen the page.

"King Sound," he said, scanning her face. "You found the entry."

She hesitated. "He wrote about someone, a woman he left behind."

Dante's jaw tightened. "Elara."

The name hit the air like a blade dropped in still water.

"You know her?" Ava asked, startled.

"She was Anderson's wife," Dante said quietly. "Or so the stories claim. A pearl diver. Some say she drowned when he went north. Others say she vanished on the tide and was never seen again. But Anderson believed she lived."

He gestured towards the journal. "That passage, it is the first reference to what he called the Map of Bones. Not just a chart of treasure, but a trail of what he left behind, pieces of himself. His fortune, his sins, and his love."

Ava's fingers tightened on the book. "You think she is connected to the treasure?"

"I think," Dante said slowly, "that Anderson left his heart buried along with it. And if what we found on Middle Island is any sign, the next clue is not gold. It is blood."

The ship creaked as the morning wind shifted. Dante spread out the pages Ava had copied from the chest they had uncovered on Middle Island, faded maps, strange markings, and symbols carved into parchment that looked more like bone than paper.

One symbol caught Ava's eye, a spiral intersected by three stars. It was etched beside the words:

Return to the Sound. Where the pearl sleeps beneath the ribs of the sea.

She frowned. "That is near King Sound, near where he said he left her."

Dante nodded. "The ribs of the sea could mean the reef line. Or a shipwreck. Maybe both."

Ava touched the spiral. "He was not mapping gold, was he? He was mapping her."

For a moment, silence stretched between them, charged and heavy. Dante's gaze lingered on her, and something unspoken passed there, recognition, maybe even fear.

"You feel it, don't you?" he said finally. "That pull. Like the sea knows you."

Ava did not answer. She did not need to. The truth thudded in her chest like a heartbeat. She had always known the tides too well, the way they turned and whispered, the way storms seemed to rise and fall with her moods. Even her father had said it once. You are salt-born, Ava. The ocean's in your blood.

Now, she wondered if it was more than a metaphor.

That night, as they sailed northwest, the stars wheeled bright above them. Ava sat on the foredeck, the journal open across her knees. She read by lantern light, the sea whispering against the hull.

Another passage bled through the page:

The pearl is not a stone but a heart. I carved it for her, from bone and salt, from what the sea left of me. It belongs to her blood. Not mine. Never mine.

A shiver ran down her spine.

"If she finds it, she will remember who she is. If she does not, it will remember her."

Dante joined her quietly, crouching beside the lantern. "You found more?"

Ava nodded. "Anderson did not just bury a treasure. He created something. Something alive."

He studied the ink, his brow furrowed. "A pearl carved from bone? That is impossible."

"Is it?" Ava whispered. "Or is that what we have been chasing all along?"

She looked up, and the starlight caught in her eyes, flecks of silver and blue, like the ocean reflecting itself. Dante stared for a long moment, realisation dawning like a shadow crossing the sun.

"Ava," he said, voice low. "What if it's not just a legend? What if you are the one Anderson was writing about?"

She laughed softly, but there was no humour in it. "Two centuries late for reincarnation, don't you think?"

"Not reincarnation," he said, shaking his head. "Inheritance."

He reached out, brushing his thumb along the edge of the open page, where Anderson's ink had faded to rust red. "Anderson's line vanished after he disappeared. No heirs. No trace. But if Elara survived, if she carried a child before he left…"

The words hung there, heavy and unreal.

Ava swallowed. "You think I'm descended from her?"

"I think," Dante said slowly, "that you've been called here for a reason. That this," he tapped the journal, "was not meant for me to find. It was meant for you."

The sea groaned softly under the hull, and a streak of lightning flashed on the horizon. Ava closed the journal and stared into the distance, heart pounding.

Her father's voice echoed in memory, the stories he told by firelight, the way he always avoided questions about her mother's side of the family.

A mother who died young. A father who never explained how they came to Esperance. A name that did not match any record she could find.

Now, everything felt as if it were shifting beneath her feet, as though the ocean itself were pulling her towards the truth.

The pearl is not a stone but a heart.

It belongs to her blood.

The wind rose, cold and sharp, carrying the faintest whisper, not words, not quite sound, but something older, deeper.

And for the first time, Ava was not sure if she was chasing Anderson's treasure, or if it was chasing her.

Chapter Nineteen:
The Weight of Water

The world had gone eerily still.

The Reaver slid through the open water like a ghost, her black hull whispering secrets the sea refused to share. A thin fog pressed low over the waves, swallowing the horizon. Even the gulls were gone.

Ava stood at the rail, Anderson's journal clutched in her hands. The leather was slick with salt and sweat, her thumb tracing the warped seam like she could rub sense into it, or herself.

She couldn't shake Dante's look from earlier. The one that had lingered a moment too long when she caught him watching her, his eyes not of a captain, but of a man measuring something he didn't understand, or something he was hiding.

The silence gnawed at her.

Below deck, she found him where she knew he'd be, hunched over his charts again, a bottle half drained beside him. The cabin was thick with smoke and lamplight, the air heavy with the tang of rum and restraint.

He didn't look up. "You should be sleeping."

"I can't."

"Nightmares?"

She took a step closer. "You tell me."

That made him glance up, one brow raised. "What is that supposed to mean?"

Ava's jaw tightened. "It means I am done being kept in the dark."

He leaned back in his chair, feigning ease, but the tension in his shoulders betrayed him. "You've been reading again."

"You keep saying that like it's a sin."

"Because you read too much into things you don't understand."

Ava's laugh was sharp, humourless. "Maybe that's because no one will explain them to me."

His expression hardened, but she didn't stop.

"You knew something was different about me. From the start."

"I didn't—"

"Don't," she snapped, slamming the journal down on the table. "Don't lie to me, Dante. You brought me here for a reason. You knew I'd lead you to whatever Anderson left behind."

His eyes flicked to the journal. "That book responds to you. You think I didn't notice? The pages change when you touch them. It's like the damn sea listens to you."

Her stomach turned. "So that's it. I'm a tool. A key for your precious treasure."

Dante pushed to his feet, the chair scraping harshly against the boards. "You think I care about the treasure?"

"Of course you do!" she shouted. "It's all you've ever cared about. The maps. The coordinates. The legends. You needed me to finish Anderson's work, didn't you? That's why you kept me close, why you looked at me like that."

His face darkened. "Don't twist this."

"Oh, I'm twisting?" she shot back. "You want me to believe this is something else, what? Destiny? Love?" She laughed bitterly. "You don't know what love even looks like, Dante. You only know obsession."

The words landed harder than she expected.

He flinched, not visibly, but in the quiet way a wound makes itself known.

Ava felt the heat in her chest curdle into something uglier. "You let me think I could trust you."

"I didn't let you think anything," he said, voice low, dangerous. "You chose that."

She took a step closer. "And you chose to use it."

His jaw locked, eyes burning with something between fury and regret. "I didn't plan you."

"But you used me."

"I needed you," he hissed, the words ripped from him like confession. "At first."

Her breath hitched. "At first."

Dante froze. "Ava—"

"No." She shook her head, voice cracking. "Don't say my name like that."

The silence that followed was unbearable, the kind that swells until it fills the whole room. The sea creaked around them, the lantern flickering between shadow and light.

Ava's throat burned. "Do you even know how it feels to be lied to by someone you—" She stopped herself, the word trust too small for what sat between them.

Dante stepped closer, his voice lower, rougher. "You think this is easy for me? You think I wanted to feel any of this?"

"Feel what?"

"This," he said, his hand tightening into a fist. "You. Every time I look at you, I can't think straight. The ship, the treasure, the sea, everything I've lived for feels smaller."

"Then why does it still feel like I'm nothing but a means to your end?"

He looked away, that one movement more damning than any lie.

Ava's chest tightened. "Say something," she whispered. "Say anything that proves you're not just another man chasing ghosts."

But he didn't. He stood there, rigid, jaw working, hands flexing like he was fighting the very air between them.

When he finally spoke, it was too quiet. "I don't know how."

That broke her. Not because it wasn't honest, but because it was.

She turned sharply, reaching for the door. "Then you'll lose me like he lost her," she said, her voice trembling. "And the sea will take us both."

Dante's breath caught, but he didn't move.

Ava paused at the doorway, every part of her screaming to leave, except for the small, desperate ache in her chest that made her stand there, waiting.

Waiting for him to stop her.

To grab her wrist.

To say don't go.

To say I'm sorry.

To say you mean more than all of it.

But Dante stayed frozen, the words dying somewhere between his throat and the bottle on the table.

The silence stretched so long it became an answer.

Ava swallowed hard, eyes stinging. "That's what I thought," she said, barely above a whisper. Then she left, the door clicking shut behind her.

The sound hit him harder than a storm.

Dante stood there for a long moment, staring at the empty space she'd left behind. His hand twitched, wanting to reach for the door, to pull her back, to say what he couldn't say. But his sea-born bones had never learned the language of comfort.

He'd fought storms, mutinies, and ghosts, but he didn't know how to fight this.

So he reached for the bottle instead.

He drank until the room blurred and the sea became a low hum beneath the wood.

The maps before him blurred too, lines and coordinates bleeding together like the past itself was sinking. Her name whispered through the fog of his mind, over and over, until he couldn't tell if it came from his lips or the ocean outside.

When the rum was gone, he slumped forward on the table, cheek pressed to the cool wood.

The journal lay open beside him, its pages glimmering faintly under the lamplight. New words had appeared, faint and salt-bitten. He blinked at them through the haze, barely able to focus:

The heart that follows the sea must learn to drown before it learns to love.

He let out a rough, broken laugh, the sound of a man who didn't know whether to fight or surrender.

Then, finally, silence took him too.

Journal Entry I — March 12, 1835

Wind gone nor'east again.

Elara don't talk much now. Just sits starin' out to sea like she's listenin' to it whisper.

Can't say I blame her. Sea got a voice that gets in yer bones.

She laughs less. Used to fill the deck with it, bright as sun on the swell. Now it's gone soft, like she's holdin' somethin' inside.

The men jaw 'bout gold an' ghosts, but they ain't seen what I seen.

Ain't no treasure worth her eyes when she's smilin'.

Ain't no curse meaner than leavin' her behind.

Sophie Jane

Journal Entry II — May 4, 1835

She sleeps bad now. Turns an' moans like she's fightin' the tide.

I hear her whisper, but words get lost in the wind.

She took my hand, pressed it to her belly.

Didn't say nothin', just smiled small.

Made my chest ache somethin' fierce.

Maybe she's carryin' somethin' of me.

Maybe she ain't.

Don't matter much. Sea don't let a man keep nothin' that belongs to the shore.

I told her I'd come back. Don't know if it were a lie or a prayer.

Journal Entry III — June 21, 1835

Middle Islande.

Hard rock, mean sea.

I put half the gold under the stone what points east, where mornin' light hit first.

Rest I threw to the deep. Let the sea keep her share.

Left one chest open. For her.

Men say I'm mad. Maybe I am.

But she's the only soul ever made me think there's somethin' better than this cursed life.

If she finds it, she'll know.

It weren't gold I left her. It were my heart, what the sea never let me keep.

Journal Entry IV — August 2, 1835

96

Sea's turnin' foul. Scouts in the water again, eyes like glass, watchin' me sleep.

I reckon they come for what's owed.

Told her I'd be back 'fore the full moon. Moon's near gone now.

She'll have the babe soon, if she ain't already.

Maybe boy, maybe girl. Maybe none.

World don't owe a man nothin'.

If she ever finds this book, follow the east drift 'round Middle Isle.

Look for white rock like a bone in the sand.

Dig there.

Ain't much, but it's all I got left of love.

If sea takes me, let it.

She took me long 'fore the Scouts ever did.

Journal Entry 1 —
March 12, 1835

Wind gone nor'east again.
Elara don't talk much now.
Just sits starin' out to sea
like she's listenin' to it whisper.
Can't say I blame her. Sea got
a voice that gets in yer bones.

She laughs less. Used to fill the
deck with it, bright as sun on
the swell. Now it's gone soft,
like she's holdin' somethin' inside.

The men jaw 'bout gold an' ghosts,
but they ain't seen what I seen.
Ain't no treasure worth her eyes
when she's smilin'.
Ain't no curse meaner than
leavin' her behind.

The wind had turned.

By the time The Reaver cut through the shallows, the storm was already crawling across the horizon, a bruised wall of lightning and sea mist rolling in from the west. The crew moved fast, hauling the crates from the dinghy, eyes flicking toward the dark line of boats following in the distance.

"Scouts," Isla said grimly, lowering her spyglass. "They're closing the gap."

Dante's voice cut through the roar of the surf. "Get the relics below deck. Double lash the bowline."

Ava waded through the surf beside him, breath ragged, the soaked sand sucking at her boots. "We can't outrun them in open water if the storm breaks."

"We don't need to," Dante said, his jaw set. "We just need to survive it."

They reached the deck as the first drops fell, fat, cold, and heavy. The sea hissed under the rain. The air tasted like iron.

Ava threw her soaked hair from her face, watching as Dante took the helm. His expression was carved in concentration, every muscle taut. The wind tore through the rigging, snapping the sails as the Reaver pitched forward into deeper water.

The storm came fast, faster than she had ever seen.

Lightning stitched the horizon in jagged lines. Waves rose like beasts, striking the hull with open palms. Isla shouted orders from the mast while Rafi clung to the rigging, his laughter half panic, half defiance.

And still, beneath it all, Ava heard something.

A sound too soft to be wind. Too low to be thunder.

A woman's voice.

It came through the waves like a hum at first, distant and lilting. Then words, faint, indistinct, but pulling at her bones.

Come back to the Sound… come back…

Ava froze, her eyes darting toward the sea. The water below glowed faintly, as though firelight burned beneath it.

"Dante," she called, but her voice was swallowed by the wind.

He saw her expression and followed her gaze. The water swirled around the hull, phosphorescent and unnatural. And then, just for a breath, he heard it too, that same voice, rising and fading like breath against his ear.

His hands clenched on the wheel. "Below deck!"

"No!" she shouted back. "You heard it!"

"I said below deck, Ava!"

She did not move. Her pulse thundered as she stared into the dark. Shapes flickered under the surface, not fish, not light. Something older. Something watching.

The ship lurched violently as a wave struck broadside. Ava lost her footing and Dante caught her, one arm locking around her waist. For a moment, the storm disappeared. There was only the sound of her heartbeat against his chest and the whisper of that ghostly song threading through the air.

"What is that?" she breathed.

He looked down at her, eyes burning with something fierce and terrified. "The Sound," he said. "Anderson called it that for a reason. It's not just a place, it's a call."

"From who?"

He hesitated. "From her."

Lightning split the sky, and for a heartbeat Ava saw her, a shape rising from the waves beside the ship. A woman's form, hair floating like kelp, eyes as pale as the moon. Then she was gone, lost to the rain.

The sea screamed.

By dawn, the storm had passed, but not cleanly. The deck was slick with salt and broken rope, the sails half torn, and the men too shaken to speak. Isla's knuckles were white around her spyglass.

"They've fallen back," she said. "The Scouts. Either they drowned or they turned."

"Or something else turned them," Rafi muttered.

Ava stood at the bow, hair plastered to her neck, staring at the endless grey horizon. The wind had died, but the ocean still whispered, low and rhythmic, like the echo of a heartbeat below the surface.

Dante approached, silent, his presence familiar and heavy. He stopped beside her but didn't touch her. Not yet.

"What did you see?" he asked finally.

She didn't look at him. "A woman."

He swallowed. "Describe her."

"I don't have to," she said softly. "You already know."

He didn't deny it. Couldn't.

Ava turned to him then, eyes fierce, searching. "You knew this would happen. You brought me here knowing something waited in the Sound."

His jaw tightened. "I didn't know it would call to you."

"You knew enough to fear it."

He looked away, voice low and ragged. "I feared losing you to it."

The words hung between them like mist.

The wind shifted again, carrying a faint echo, a woman's laugh, distant and heartbreakingly familiar. The crew pretended not to hear it. But Ava did. And so did Dante.

Come back to the Sound.

Ava's hand tightened on the railing. "She's not done with us."

Dante's gaze fixed on the dark water ahead. "No," he said quietly. "She never was."

Chapter Twenty:
The Ghosts of the Shore

The mainland didn't look the same any more.

They made landfall at dawn, grey skies, grey sea, grey hearts.

The storm had spent itself through the night, leaving the world washed raw. The small harbour town of Albany stretched ahead like a memory seen through fog, wharves lined with fishing boats, gulls screaming over the jetty, the faint stink of diesel and seaweed.

Ava stepped off *The Reaver* with shaking legs, her boots slipping on the slick boards. It had been weeks since she'd felt solid ground, and it didn't welcome her back gently.

Dante barked quiet orders behind her, Isla to refuel, Rafi to find supplies. He hadn't looked at her once since the storm.

Fine, she thought. Two could play that game.

The moment her feet touched the dock, she felt the weight of the world tilt. Voices. Engines. The distant clang of a bell. Everything sounded too sharp, too fast, too real.

They'd been ghosts on the water. Now, reality came back swinging.

Ava tugged her hood low and followed the dockside crowd. The air smelled of coffee and brine. A man at a fish stall shouted prices in a thick accent. Somewhere, a radio blared the local news.

Then she froze.

There, taped to a pole near the corner of the ferry terminal, was her own face.

MISSING.

AVA LAWSON, 32. LAST SEEN IN ESPERANCE.

The grainy photo had been taken from her driver's licence, smiling, normal, alive.

Her stomach turned. Someone had scrawled across the bottom in blue pen: "Reward for information. Contact Detective H. Roan."

Her heart slammed against her ribs.

She ripped the poster down, crumpled it, and shoved it into her pocket before anyone could look twice.

Ava pulled her hood tighter, forcing herself to keep walking. Every sound felt amplified, footsteps, laughter, a gull shrieking overhead. Her pulse beat so loud she thought everyone could hear it.

She passed a window and caught her reflection, salt-tangled hair, dirt smudged across her cheek, eyes too wild for the girl she used to be.

No wonder people were staring.

She wasn't missing. She was becoming someone else.

"Lawson."

The voice came from behind her, rough, uncertain.

Ava turned sharply.

A man in a hi-vis vest stood beside a fuel truck, squinting. "You're Ava Lawson, aren't you? Christ, they've been looking for you for weeks. Whole damn coast—"

Before he could finish, she bolted.

Her boots hammered the pavement as she ducked between parked cars, breath sharp and ragged. She heard the man shout after her, but the words drowned under the noise of the wharf.

She darted down a side street, heart in her throat, and pressed herself against a wall until the world stopped spinning.

For a moment, she just breathed.

Then she whispered, "Dante's gonna kill me for this."

She made her way up the hill into the heart of town. Albany's streets were waking, shops opening, shutters creaking, tourists trickling out with cameras and raincoats.

Every lamppost seemed to have her face staring back at her.

Each one a reminder of a life she'd somehow slipped out of, and wasn't sure she wanted back.

By the time she reached the Maritime Museum, her pulse had steadied but her hands hadn't. She'd been here once before, years ago, with her father. Back then, she'd thought the sea was just salt and stories. Now it whispered names.

Elara.

The sound brushed the back of her neck like a chill. She turned, but no one was there.

"Pull it together," she muttered, forcing herself towards the entrance.

The museum smelled like varnish and history. Wood floors creaked beneath her boots. Glass cases displayed relics of shipwrecks, diving bells, sextants, and weathered charts.

She drifted towards the back rooms, the ones marked Staff Only and Archival Access.

Dante's voice from last night still echoed in her head. Anderson's maps follow no logic. They're personal.

If the maps in those chests matched anything here, she could find where Anderson's story ended, and where hers began.

A guard at the front counter glanced up. Ava smiled tight and kept walking.

She slipped through a side door just as a school group poured in, the chatter covering her tracks. The hallway beyond was cool and dim, lined with old maritime photos.

At the end stood a locked glass door labelled ARCHIVE. RESTRICTED.

She tested the handle. Locked.

Ava glanced around, spotted a cleaner's trolley, and grabbed the first thing that looked remotely useful, a thin metal ruler. With a steady breath, she slid it between the latch and the frame.

Click.

Her father would've scolded her for breaking into a museum. Her mother would've asked why she didn't just ask for a key.

But neither of them were here.

And she was running out of time.

The archive smelled of dust and paper. Stacks of rolled charts filled wooden drawers labelled by date and vessel.

Ava lit her phone's torch and scanned the names:

Hesper, 1834.

Mary Anne, 1836.

Anderson's Crew, 1835.

Her pulse leapt. She tugged the drawer open.

Inside were brittle logs, wrapped in linen and labelled in faded ink. The first was a manifest. Jack Anderson.

She traced the name with her thumb.

He'd been here.

Right here.

She unrolled the next sheet, a map. The same symbols she'd seen carved in the cave leapt off the parchment, spirals, compass stars, a single marking near Middle Island labelled "Rising Stone."

Her breath caught.

Then another sound, footsteps in the hall.

Ava killed the light, heart hammering. She ducked behind the filing cabinet as a torch beam swept the room.

"Hello?" a man's voice called. "Anyone back here?"

Ava held her breath, clutching the rolled map to her chest.

The beam lingered, then disappeared. The door shut again.

She exhaled, slow and shaky. "Too close."

When she slipped out a few minutes later, the map was hidden under her jacket.

Rain had started to fall again, thin and silver.

She turned down the narrow lane behind the museum, cutting between the bins. A figure stepped from the shadows ahead.

Dante.

His eyes found hers, cold and furious.

"What the hell were you thinking?"

"I found something," she said.

"You disappeared."

"You weren't exactly talking to me."

He stepped closer, lowering his voice. "You've got half the coast looking for you, and you stroll into a government building like it's a Sunday market?"

"I told you I can take care of myself."

"Not from this," he growled, pulling a crumpled poster from his coat, her face staring up from it, wet and warped by the rain.

Ava stared at it, throat tight. "I didn't ask to be saved."

"No," he said, eyes dark. "But you keep getting lost."

Thunder rolled again in the distance, not from the sea this time, but inland, heavy and low.

Ava turned away, swallowing the lump in her throat. "I found one of Anderson's maps," she said, voice shaking. "It matches the ones we took from Middle Island. The marks, they line up with the coast. There's another site, near the Sound."

Dante's anger faltered, replaced by the same haunted look he'd worn in the storm. "You sure?"

She met his gaze. "Elara's voice. It led me here."

He flinched. "Don't start with that again."

"She's not haunting me," Ava said quietly. "She's guiding me."

Dante's jaw clenched. "You don't know that."

"I feel it."

Rain streaked between them. For a heartbeat, the city noise faded, just the two of them standing in the narrow alley, ghosts of their own making.

Then Isla's voice echoed from the far end. "They found us!"

A black van turned the corner onto the wharf road, two men in plain clothes climbing out, scanning the street. One pointed directly toward them.

Ava cursed under her breath. "Detectives."

"Move," Dante ordered.

They ran.

Through the alley, down the steps, across the soaked pavement toward the docks. Ava's heart pounded in time with her footsteps. Behind them, shouts cut through the rain.

They ducked behind a row of shipping crates, pressed close against the corrugated metal. Ava's pulse roared in her ears.

"Rafi's ready to cast off," Isla hissed into her comm from the boat. "Thirty seconds."

Dante grabbed Ava's wrist and pulled her after him. They sprinted across the pier just as a shout went up behind them. A bullet hit the water beside the hull with a sharp hiss.

Ava didn't look back.

They leapt onto *The Reaver* as the engines roared to life. Rafi gunned it hard, the boat veering out into open water.

The rain came down in sheets now, turning the world into a blur of motion and sound. Ava clutched the rail, breathing hard, watching the shoreline fade into grey.

Dante stood beside her, soaked to the bone, jaw tight as he stared ahead.

"Next time you decide to play archaeologist," he said, voice low, "maybe tell me before the police get involved."

Ava smirked faintly. "You'd have said no."

"You're damn right."

She looked at him then, really looked, the anger, the exhaustion, the fear beneath both. "You'd have stopped me," she said softly. "Like you always try to."

He didn't answer.

Somewhere behind them, thunder rolled again, and beneath it, just barely, a whisper that only she could hear.

Follow the stone that points to the sun.

Ava's hand closed around the stolen map beneath her jacket. The paper was damp, but the ink was still clear. The coordinates glimmered faintly under the deck lights, the next trail Anderson had left behind.

She looked toward the horizon, where the dark outline of King Sound waited beneath the clouds.

"Then that's where we go next," she murmured.

And as *The Reaver* disappeared into the rain, the mainland, and the world that still thought she was missing, fell away behind her once more.

Chapter Twenty One:
The Chase

The sea was no longer quiet.

It screamed.

The horizon broke into chaos, the dark outlines of four Scout boats slicing through the morning glare, white wakes burning behind them like scars across the water. Their engines howled over the wind, closing fast.

"Three boats closing port side! One behind!" Isla shouted, voice barely audible over the roar of the engines.

Dante spun the wheel hard. *The Reaver* tilted, spray exploding over the deck. The air filled with salt and smoke.

Ava clung to the railing, her knuckles white. She clasped the pendant in her pocket. She couldn't lose it.

Rafi ducked behind the wheelhouse, loading rounds into the rifle. "They're better armed than last time!"

"Then aim better," Dante barked, voice sharp as cut glass.

The first volley came, gunfire cracking over the water, bullets slamming into the hull. The sound was deafening, metallic, raw. Ava hit the deck as a round punched through the railing inches from her face.

"Jesus," she gasped.

Dante was already there, shoving her down behind a crate. "Stay low!"

"Where are they coming from?"

"Everywhere!"

Spray exploded as a Scout boat swung close on the port side. Men in dark jackets leaned out, shouting, their rifles flashing.

Rafi fired back, two sharp cracks that echoed across the water. One of the Scouts staggered, fell overboard. The others ducked for cover.

Ava could hear her own heartbeat louder than the gunfire. The sea around them was boiling, each wave tipped with sunlight and fear.

Dante yanked the throttle forward, the boat surging ahead. "We'll lose them in the shallows!"

"Those reefs will tear us apart!" Isla yelled.

"Isla, I know what I'm doing! Just keep the port side covered!"

The Reaver plunged between jagged spires of coral, the water turning from blue to pale jade. The hull scraped once, hard, throwing Ava against the deck.

Pain shot through her ribs. She groaned, rolling to her side.

Dante reached for her, eyes dark with something that wasn't just fear. "You hurt?"

"Just bruised," she rasped.

"Stay with me."

"Where else would I go?"

Another explosion, this one closer. The stern shuddered, smoke curling into the air.

"They hit the engine housing!" Rafi shouted.

"Keep us moving!" Dante ordered. "We're not stopping!"

He spun the wheel again, cutting between two reefs so tight the hull screamed. Salt spray blinded them, the air thick with gunpowder and adrenaline.

Ava crawled toward the railing, peering out. One of the Scout boats had clipped the reef, its bow crumpled, men shouting as it listed.

She couldn't help the grim satisfaction that flickered through her chest.

But the others were still coming.

The sound of gunfire thinned for a moment, just the thrum of the engine and the slap of water. Then something heavy hit the deck with a metallic clang.

Ava turned, a grapple hook.

Before she could react, two Scouts swung over the side. One lunged at her, boots slipping on the wet deck.

She rolled, instinct kicking in, and swung the nearest thing she could grab, a rusted wrench. It connected with the man's jaw, sending him sprawling.

The second Scout caught her arm, twisting hard. Pain shot through her shoulder.

Dante's roar cut through the chaos. He was there in seconds, tackling the man into the railing. The two struggled, fists flying.

Ava scrambled backward, gasping, her vision blurring.

"Stay behind me!" Dante shouted, shoving the attacker into the sea.

The moment he turned, another shot rang out. Dante staggered, a spray of blood from his upper arm.

"Dante!"

He gritted his teeth, pressing his hand to the wound. "It's fine."

"It's not—"

"I said it's fine!" he snapped, the fury in his voice hiding the pain.

Something broke inside her then, fear, love, frustration all twisted into one unbearable knot.

"Stop acting like this doesn't scare you!" she yelled. "Like I don't—"

Another round whizzed between them, splintering the mast.

"Later!" he shouted. "You want to talk about feelings? Survive first!"

They hit open water again. Behind them, one Scout boat burned, another spun in circles with its engine dead. But two still followed, relentless.

The clouds above had darkened, rolling low and heavy. Lightning flashed across the horizon.

Rafi cursed under his breath. "Storm's turning east. If we stay in the channel, it'll trap us!"

Dante's voice was raw. "Then we take the inside passage."

Isla's head snapped up. "That's suicide!"

"Not if we're faster."

Ava caught the look in his eyes, desperation edged with something darker.

"Dante—" she started.

"Trust me," he said, spinning the wheel.

She wanted to scream at him. Instead, she braced herself as *The Reaver* roared toward the narrowing mouth of the channel.

Rain hit like needles. The world blurred into motion, white water, grey sky, black shapes closing behind them.

Gunfire flashed again, the muzzle flares like sparks in the storm. One bullet tore through the canvas above, another hit the deck inches from Isla's hand.

"Down!" Dante bellowed.

Ava ducked as another round ricocheted off the railing. The air reeked of smoke and salt.

Rafi leaned out, firing blind. "We can't keep this up!"

Dante's voice was steady but low. "We don't have to."

Ahead, the reefs split into two narrow passages. He took the left one without hesitation.

Ava could feel the shift, the boat scraping rock, the current doubling in strength.

"Depth's dropping!" Isla shouted.

"Hold her steady!"

Then, with a sound like tearing metal, the hull clipped something unseen. *The Reaver* lurched sideways.

Ava lost her footing.

The world tilted, her shoulder slammed into the railing, and before she could grab hold, the next wave hit.

It lifted her clean off her feet.

Dante shouted her name.

Then the sea swallowed her.

The cold hit like a knife. Salt filled her mouth, her nose, her lungs. She kicked, disoriented, breaking the surface long enough to see chaos, the boat spinning, gunfire flashing.

"AVA!" Dante's voice was a roar through the storm.

She tried to swim, but the current dragged her under again, spinning her toward the wreckage of one of the Scout boats.

Hands grabbed her, rough, gloved, pulling her up. She gasped, coughing seawater, as a voice barked in her ear.

"Got her! Pull her in!"

A black hood came down over her head before she could scream.

"Let me go!" she thrashed, but the grip only tightened. The world shrank to the sound of engines and the rain beating on metal.

On *The Reaver*, Dante was already turning the boat. His bleeding arm left streaks across the wheel.

Rafi shouted something, but he didn't hear it.

All he could see was the place where she'd fallen, the sea boiling, the echo of her name still on the wind.

"Come on, come on," he muttered, voice cracking. "Not her. Not again."

Lightning split the sky, revealing the Scout vessel speeding away with a figure slumped on deck.

"Ava," he breathed.

Rafi grabbed his shoulder. "We'll never catch them in this storm—"

"Like hell we won't!" Dante snarled, shoving the throttle forward.

The Reaver lurched, engines screaming. The hull groaned under the strain.

Rain blinded him, blood soaking through his sleeve. But he didn't care.

He'd seen that look before, the sea taking someone he couldn't save.

Not again.

The chase stretched into the night. The Scout vessel wove between rocks and shoals, its lights flickering through the rain.

Dante followed, every muscle screaming, every wave a punishment. The storm howled like the ghosts of the Sound.

Rafi fired into the dark, sparks flying. One of the Scout's engines sputtered, smoke rising.

"Hit!" Isla shouted.

Dante pushed harder. "Bring us alongside!"

The hulls slammed together, wood against metal, grinding. Dante leapt, rope in hand, catching the Scout's rail.

"Dante, no!" Isla yelled.

He didn't listen. He swung over the gap, boots hitting the wet deck. A Scout turned, raising his rifle — Dante tackled him, the weapon skidding away.

Rain drenched them both as they fought, every hit echoing through the storm.

Then he saw her.

Ava, bound, hood half torn, eyes wide and furious.

"Get down!" Dante shouted.

He grabbed the nearest man, slammed him against the mast, and fired the pistol he'd stolen. The flash lit the rain in silver. The Scout dropped.

Dante rushed to her, cutting the ropes.

"You came," she whispered, voice raw.

He caught her face in his hands, rain and blood mixing on their skin. "You think I'd let the sea take you?"

Her breath hitched. "You could've died."

"I'd rather drown with you than watch you disappear."

Something inside her broke open — fear, fury, love — all tangled together.

But before either could speak again, the deck tilted. The Scout vessel struck a reef, wood splintering.

Dante pulled her toward the railing. "Jump!"

They leapt as the ship buckled, crashing into the waves.

The sea swallowed them whole.

When Ava opened her eyes again, she was lying on the deck of *The Reaver*, rain pounding her face.

Dante hovered above her, soaked, bleeding, his expression unreadable.

"You're insane," she whispered.

He laughed once, hoarse and broken. "You say that like it's news."

Her hand found his, trembling. "You really came for me."

He met her eyes, voice low. "I'll always come for you."

The storm still raged around them, but for the first time, Ava didn't hear fear in the wind, only promise.

Behind them, the wreckage burned on the horizon, a scar of fire against the dark.

Ahead, the Sound stretched wide and black, full of ghosts, secrets, and the unbroken pull of the sea.

Ava turned toward it, her hand tightening around his.

"Then let's finish what Anderson started," she said.

And for once, Dante didn't argue.

Chapter Twenty Two:
The Sound Between Hearts

The storm died as quickly as it had risen.

By dawn, the sea lay heavy and swollen, waves lapping at a narrow stretch of sand that could barely be called an island.

The Reaver sat half-beached on the far side, her hull split along the lower deck, one mast snapped clean in two. The smell of fuel and salt hung in the still air.

Ava woke to the sound of gulls. Her body ached, her head throbbed, and every breath scraped her ribs raw. The last thing she remembered was Dante's voice and the sea tearing her from him again.

Now he was there, sitting near her, silent, soaked, eyes hollow.

He hadn't slept.

"You're alive," he said quietly, voice rough from shouting and smoke.

"Barely," she managed. "Where are we?"

"North side of King Sound. Some kind of cay. Uncharted."

She tried to sit, wincing. "Is everyone—"

"Rafi's working on the engines. Isla…" He hesitated, glancing toward the dunes. "She hasn't said much since we pulled you out."

Ava's chest tightened. "She saw?"

"She thought you were gone."

The sand was warm under her feet as she crossed toward the dunes. Isla sat near the wreck of a lifeboat, knees drawn up, hair plastered to her face, staring at the horizon.

Ava stopped a few paces away. "You should be resting."

Isla didn't move. "Could say the same for you."

Ava sank down beside her, the silence stretching between them, thick with everything unspoken.

For the first time since they'd met, Isla looked small, fragile in a way Ava had never seen. The tough, quick-witted girl who'd faced gunfire without blinking now looked like a child lost at sea.

"I thought you were dead," Isla said finally, voice low. "When you went overboard… I saw the water close over you. I couldn't do anything."

Ava swallowed hard. "You didn't lose me."

Isla shook her head. "I did. For a minute that felt like forever. And I realised—" She broke off, wiping her cheek roughly with the back of her hand. "You're my anchor out here. Without you… I don't know what I'd be holding onto."

Ava reached out, squeezing her hand. "You held the crew together while Dante nearly tore himself apart. That's something."

Isla gave a weak laugh, half a sob. "He went mad, you know. Storm or not, he was going after them. Rafi tried to stop him. I thought he'd kill us all trying to get to you."

Ava felt the world tilt again, the weight of what she'd cost them pressing heavy on her chest. "He shouldn't have."

Isla turned, eyes fierce through her tears. "Don't say that. He had to. I've seen the way he looks at you, Ava. Like the sea would split in two if he told it to."

Ava blinked, her heart stuttering. "That's not—"

"It is," Isla cut in, a small smile ghosting through the exhaustion. "And maybe that's the only reason we made it back."

They sat for a while, saying nothing. The waves rolled in soft and slow, hissing against the sand.

Finally, Isla looked at her again. "You scared the hell out of me."

Ava smiled faintly. "Then we're even."

Behind them, the steady rhythm of hammering echoed through the morning.

Rafi knelt near the hull, stripped to his waist, shoulders slick with sweat and salt. He worked with quiet determination, every movement deliberate.

"How bad is it?" Ava asked, approaching.

Rafi glanced up, exhaustion etched deep in his face. "Portside intake's shot. Engine casing's cracked. We'll be lucky if she limps."

"Can we patch it?"

He shrugged. "If we can find resin and a miracle."

Ava crouched beside him, tracing the split seam with her fingers. "You've done worse."

"Yeah," Rafi muttered. "But not after a gunfight, a storm, and a damn rescue mission that nearly killed half the crew."

She opened her mouth to answer, but his tone softened first. "Don't get me wrong, Lawson. I'd have done the same. But next time, try not to make it so dramatic, yeah?"

Ava laughed, weak but real. "No promises."

He grinned, shaking his head. "Figures."

By midday, the heat rose off the sand in shimmering waves. They'd built a makeshift shelter using torn canvas and driftwood. The air smelled of diesel, salt, and smoke.

Dante stayed apart from them, sitting near the prow of the wreck, eyes fixed on the sea. His arm was bandaged, his face shadowed. Every so often, he flexed his hand like he couldn't believe it was still attached.

Ava watched him from the shade, feeling the pull between them like a tide she couldn't fight.

"You should talk to him," Isla murmured, following her gaze.

"He's not ready."

Isla arched a brow. "He nearly died for you. I'd say that counts as 'ready.'"

Ava looked down, fingers tracing the sand. "Maybe he doesn't know why he did it."

"Then make him figure it out."

When the sun began to sink, Ava walked to the edge of the surf. The tide licked at her boots, cool and steady. Dante didn't look up when she stopped beside him.

"You should rest," she said softly.

"So should you."

They stood in silence, watching the water shift from gold to bruised violet.

Finally, Ava spoke. "I heard you."

His jaw tightened. "When?"

"When I went over. You called my name."

He exhaled, rough and uneven. "I thought I'd lost you."

"You almost did."

He turned then, eyes burning with something that cut straight through her. "You don't understand. When I saw them take you, it was like the ocean was repeating history. Anderson… Elara… every curse tied to this damn ship."

"Then why save me?" she whispered.

"Because I couldn't let it happen again."

The words hung between them, raw and heavy.

She stepped closer, the surf curling around their ankles. "You think fate's repeating itself?"

"I don't know what to think," he said, voice cracking. "All I know is I've spent my life trying not to care about anything I couldn't keep. And then you came aboard."

Her chest tightened. "And now?"

He looked at her, rain-coloured eyes filled with too many storms. "Now I'm terrified of what happens if I lose you again."

The air between them felt fragile. One breath too deep and it would shatter.

Ava's voice was barely a whisper. "Then don't."

They didn't move for a long time. The sea hissed against the sand, steady, timeless.

Behind them, Isla and Rafi had lit a small fire near the shelter. The smell of smoke drifted on the wind.

When Ava finally turned, Isla was watching from the dunes, not intruding, just making sure she was there. Their eyes met, and for a moment, no words were needed.

Isla's small nod said everything. *We made it. You're safe. We're still us.*

Later that night, as the others slept, Ava sat alone near the dying fire. The pendant hung heavy around her neck, the metal warm from her skin. She turned it over in her fingers, tracing the engraved spiral.

The waves whispered against the shore, soft, rhythmic, hypnotic.

Then she heard it.

Ava.

The voice was faint, carried on the wind, soft and sorrowful, like a sigh between worlds.

He left me here. But you will find what I could not.

Her heart hammered. She looked toward the horizon, where the dark line of the mainland glimmered under the moon.

"Elara?" she whispered.

The Sound remembers. The sea keeps what love cannot.

A tear slipped down her cheek. "Why me?"

The voice faded with the wind, leaving only silence and the endless hush of waves.

Ava closed her hand around the pendant. The spiral seemed to hum faintly against her skin, a pulse, a promise.

By morning, the weather had turned again. A hot wind swept in from the north, carrying the smell of rain. Rafi was already on his feet, checking the patched engine lines.

"She'll float," he said, voice hoarse. "Won't be pretty, but she'll move."

Isla tossed him a canteen. "You're a miracle worker."

He grinned. "Miracle's a strong word. Let's call it stubbornness."

Ava joined them, pulling her hair back with a strip of cloth. "How long before she's ready?"

"Couple of hours," Rafi said. "If the tide doesn't shift too soon."

Dante emerged from the shadows of the broken mast, his arm still bandaged but his expression sharper, purpose replacing exhaustion.

"Then we make it count," he said. "We're heading east, along the coast. Anderson's notes point to another marker near the mouth of the Sound. That's where the real trail starts."

Ava met his gaze. "And if the Scouts are still out there?"

His lips curved into something that wasn't quite a smile. "Then they'll have to catch us again."

Isla groaned. "Not funny."

"Didn't say it was," Dante muttered.

Rafi chuckled under his breath. "Same crew, same madness."

"Same heart," Ava added softly.

They all looked at her, tired, battered, but alive. The bond between them, forged through storms and blood and salt, felt unbreakable now.

Even the sea seemed to listen.

As they pushed *The Reaver* back into the shallows, the clouds began to part, streaks of sunlight spilling across the water. The tide lifted, gentle at first, then stronger, as if the ocean itself wanted them to move forward.

Ava stood at the bow once more, hand resting on the railing. Isla joined her, their shoulders brushing.

"Next time," Isla murmured, "try not to get kidnapped."

Ava laughed. "No promises."

"Good," Isla said, smiling faintly. "I'd miss the drama."

They watched as the Sound opened before them, vast, shimmering, filled with ghosts and light. Somewhere beneath those depths, Anderson's final secret waited.

And this time, Ava knew she wouldn't face it alone.